TORY HEAVEN

or

THUNDER ON THE RIGHT

Persephone Book N° 128
Published by Persephone Books Ltd 2018

© Estate of Marghanita Laski

Preface © David Kynaston

First published in 1948

This edition is a facsimile of the 1949 USA edition.

Endpapers taken from 'Transport', a 1945 dress fabric in
printed rayon crêpe designed by Feliks Topolski for Ascher Ltd
© V & A Images.

Typeset in ITC Baskerville by
Keystroke, Wolverhampton

Printed and bound in Germany by
GGP Media GmbH, Poessneck

978 191 0263 181

Persephone Books Ltd
59 Lamb's Conduit Street
London WC1N 3NB
020 7242 9292

www.persephonebooks.co.uk

TORY HEAVEN

or

THUNDER ON THE RIGHT

by

MARGHANITA LASKI

✳✳✳✳✳✳✳

with a new preface by

DAVID KYNASTON

PERSEPHONE BOOKS
LONDON

PREFACE

****

'Quite a number of the original upper middle class Kensingtonians survive,' noted the writer John Brophy in April 1948, as he looked about him at Derry & Toms and elsewhere. 'All over sixty, now, some over eighty. Most of the men are bewildered and defeated. The old ladies are invincible. Neither rationing, queues, the disappearance of servants, nor heavy taxation and the lowered purchasing power of money gets them down: the unforeseen bad times gives them something to talk clichés about.' These old dears mainly took their meals in restaurants, talking to each other across the small tables 'as though from mountain top to mountain top'. They were also, observed Brophy with grudging admiration, 'quite unscrupulous': 'They were born to privilege, and in the days of their decline they fight for it. Given half a chance, any one of them will sail in ahead of the longest bus queue.'

During those difficult years after the Labour Party's landslide victory in July 1945 – years of daily austerity almost worse than during the war itself – it sometimes seemed that the middle class, comprising at most a quarter of the population, grumbled for England. Take two correspondents to the *Evening Standard* (the most upmarket of London's three evening papers) in April 1947. 'Before the war,' complained one, 'we could afford to go abroad for holidays. Last year we imposed ourselves upon relatives. We used to play golf, tennis and badminton. How can we afford them now?' A grammar-school master was only marginally less miserable: 'We could give up the car; but we cling to it as a last link with comfort and luxury, having surrendered so many other things, including annual holidays, library subscriptions and golf.' Already it was becoming almost axiomatic that it was the middle class that had taken the biggest hit since the war – and crucially, it was not just an economic hit, but psychological as well, with a growing feeling that they had somehow been muscled out of the picture by the hitherto patronised-cum-despised working class. 'It is very noticeable that nowadays the well-fed, well-clad, sweetly smiling bourgeoisie male & female have disappeared from poster and advertisement,' reflected another teacher, Gladys Langford, in her diary in May 1947. 'It is the broadly grinning and obviously unwashed "worker" who appears in more than life size on our hoardings and Tube stations.'

It was obvious enough which political party stood to benefit from an increasingly aggrieved middle class. In the summer of 1948, almost exactly three years after the shock of defeat, a memo from the Conservative Party's Research Department set out what it hoped would be the next election's battle-ground: 'The floating vote is mainly middle class (incomes £700–£1,200 per annum). These people are now finding it

****

impossible to live. The chief fear of the middle-class voter is being submerged by a more prosperous working class. Our whole appeal must be in this direction.' Back in 1945, much of the middle-of-the-road or faintly progressive middle class had voted Labour for the first time in their lives. The question by 1948 was whether it was also going to be the last time.

Marghanita Laski's *Tory Heaven* appeared that April, the same month as Brophy's field research in Kensington. Advertised by the Cresset Press as an 'exquisite fantasy', and 'as amusing and gay as *Love on the Supertax*' (her wartime novel), it had a clear political agenda – being aimed squarely at those in the middle class who by now were starting to long for the overthrow of Clement Attlee's government and a return to the familiar Tory certainties of social hierarchy, of rigid class distinctions, and of almost unquestioned privilege and entitlement for those born on the right side of the tracks. With a light but deadly touch, Laski evokes a counter-factual world in which (in the words of Hugh Fausset in the *Manchester Guardian*) 'the most reactionary Tories have come to power and re-created a class-system in which everyone is graded with feudal exactitude and all the picturesque trappings of the eighteenth century are artificially restored'. For all her palpable design, she is too subtle and elegant a writer to express her own horror at this grotesque turning back of the clock. Instead, like the best political satirists from Swift to Orwell, she leaves it entirely to others to draw out the lessons of her story. Or as Ralph Straus put it in the *Sunday Times*: 'Conservatives with high blood pressure are advised not to read it.'

****

One of the most telling episodes is when the central character, the hero/anti-hero James Leigh-Smith, newly returned to England and delighted to have been allocated (as a 'public-school man') Grade A status, visits his parents in Hindhead. The father being a stockbroker, they are likewise Grade A, but seem increasingly unhappy about the state of things since the Tory *coup d'état*. James asks him why. 'I suppose it was partly the war,' explains a cogitating Leigh-Smith senior. 'We found ourselves mixing with all sorts of peculiar people then, and the funny thing was, we rather liked it.' Not least the socially jumbled experience of the Home Guard: 'A rare old time we used to have together. Even after the war was over, we all used to meet at that pub down the road for a pint and a good chin-wag.' Under the implacable Tory regime, however, any such mixing is strictly forbidden. 'We've got to stick to our class. That's the law. If we don't, we're liable to get degraded.' Laski's message, here and throughout the novel, is twofold: not only that the war had acted as an entirely beneficial solvent in the breaking down of class barriers, but that in Britain an authoritarian regime was as likely to emerge from the right as from the left.

The latter point was especially timely (and in our populist/nationalist era perhaps still has contemporary relevance). Winston Churchill in the 1945 election had sought to equate a future Labour government with the murderous tyranny of the Gestapo; while that same year, George Orwell's *Animal Farm* had, for all its undeniable justice in relation to Stalinism, provided easy propaganda points for the right. Another telling scene comes towards the novel's end, after James's

****

elderly, well-bred friend, Ughtred, is unable at Paddington station to buy a copy of the *Spectator* or the *New Statesman*, both of them shut down by government. 'I have always been a Conservative,' he tells James. 'I have always believed in Privilege. I have always believed in the natural superiority of one class and that my own; I have always believed that this class alone was by nature fitted to govern. But equally I have always believed, fundamentally and decisively, in the freedom of the British Press.' To James's consternation as well as incomprehension ('they'd all be putting forward progressive views and then you'd never have a sound Tory Government'), Ughtred on these grounds breaks decisively with the regime, in the process forfeiting all his deeply cherished rights as a full-time London clubman.

If Laski's prime agenda was political (befitting a niece of Harold Laski, leading political theorist and recent chairman of the Labour Party), she also may well have had in her sights a high-profile literary target. 'A clever though reliably conventional school friend rebuked me for never having heard of Angela Thirkell,' the critic and novelist David Pryce-Jones has recalled of his boarding school in the immediate post-war period. '"At home we think she's the best living author. Everyone reads her." Home was in Camberley.' Thirkell's hatred of what she saw as the socialist destruction of old England struck a deep chord, and during these years her 'Barsetshire' sequence of novels sold prodigiously. The most recent, at the time Laski was writing, was *Private Enterprise* (1947), as usual set among the acutely class-conscious minor gentry of Trollope's fictional county. In it, Thirkell discerned

✳✳✳✳✳✳✳✳✳

after a year or so of peace 'a great increase of boredom and crossness, which made people wonder what use it had been to stand alone against the Powers of Darkness if the reward was to be increasing discomfort and a vast army of half-baked bureaucrats stifling all freedom and ease'. In literary terms, Thirkell did not perhaps *quite* deserve the lofty Pryce-Jones put-down; but in human-cum-political terms, both her tone and message had become by this time unattractively narrow and blinkered. *Tory Heaven* is in a very real sense the anti-Thirkell – and seven decades later, it has (in horse-racing parlance) stayed on appreciably the stronger.

Was it also – painful thought though this is – a riposte to a much-loved Persephone author? 'The Exiles' was the title of a story by Mollie Panter-Downes that appeared in the *New Yorker* in October 1947 and was subsequently collected in *Minnie's Room*, Persephone Book no. 34. Told with all her usual acute human understanding, it relates the final weeks of a retired colonel and his wife before they leave London and emigrate to South Africa. 'Arthur felt Things very keenly, she would say,' when people asked why they were leaving. 'As she spoke, Things seemed to assume the shape of a dragon that was now firmly couched in its lair beneath the hitherto benign towers of Westminster. This dragon, she implied, was out to devour the Stanburys and their kind, to gobble their modest, honourable incomes, to push them to the wall and bar every path with the lashings of its hideously powerful tail. In time, Arthur felt, the monster of Things would get the whole country down. . .' 'Things', Panter-Downes hardly needed to spell out, meant the Labour government and its monstrous regiment of bureaucrats implementing every socialist wish. The colonel also identifies a fundamental moral decay under the new order. 'There was no honesty left in the people,' he is described as telling his barber, 'there were no manners, there was nothing but this new, slipshod idea of working the shortest possible hours for the largest possible wage.' The reader is left to sympathise with the couple as they make their reluctant exile, and at no point does Panter-Downes distance herself from their bitterness. Of course, it is no more than a punt that her story influenced *Tory Heaven* – which, after all, was published only six months later. But at the least, it is a further indication of the embattled middle-class mood that Laski was seeking to counteract.

Laski's highly engaging, beautifully written novel – the work of someone long immersed in Jane Austen (a nod to her in the central character's name?) – was only sparsely reviewed by the English press. Straus thought it 'wickedly amusing', Fausset called it 'an ingeniously contrived and wittily told tale', but most papers and magazines ignored it. There was a greater response in the States, where it was published under the unhelpful title *Toasted English*, yet presumably it was in her own country that Laski would have hoped for the major impact. In February 1950, less than two years after *Tory Heaven*'s appearance, a general election saw Labour's majority cut savagely; and in October 1951, the Tories under Churchill resumed their accustomed seats of power. In both cases, the middle class returned *en masse* to its traditional allegiance. Thirkell, cousin to Stanley Baldwin and Rudyard Kipling, had won the immediate political if not the literary battle.

This edition of Laski's novel is a facsimile of the American edition: partly because it is set more generously (no paper rationing there), partly also because it has a fuller, more satisfying ending than in the original English version. I will not give away the denouement to the story. But suffice here to say that, as with so many privileged and well-educated people, James really should have thought harder about which side he was on and the true meaning of *noblesse oblige*.

David Kynaston, London 2017

TORY HEAVEN

or

THUNDER ON THE RIGHT

Chapter 1

IT IS DIFFICULT after the passage of years to recall the precise emotions with which the population of England switched on their radio sets one summer evening in 1945 and prepared to hear that the Tories had won the General Election. It is even harder to enter into the feelings of five British subjects marooned on an island in the inscrutable East awaiting news of the elected governors who were to lead the destinies of the distant nation, to which they hoped — with luck — soon to return.

They had all escaped together from Singapore. Chance had united them at the same quayside, had tumbled them into the same launch, had omitted to endow any of them with any sense of navigation. Chance had led them to the Swiss Family Robinson's island just off New Guinea; Father and Mother Robinson had long since died out, and the descendants of Fritz, Ernest, Jack and Franz were running successful hotels in the Engadine, the Grindelwald, the Ticino, and one, indeed, in Wilwaukee, Wisconsin; but the far-seeing patriarch had so well and conveniently stocked his island before his demise at the age of one hundred and three that all amenities incumbent on comfortable living were to be found there. These included, fortunately, a store of tinned foods and a tin-opener; else,

1

the other conveniences might have gone for nothing, for none of our party could cook.

This was composed as follows:

First, our hero, James Leigh-Smith. After reading for a Pass Degree at Oxford, James had, after some brief spells raising coffee in Brazil, sheep in the Argentine, and nitrates in Chili, been sent to try his luck on an uncle's rubber plantation in Malaya. His enrolment in the local defence force had not served to stay the tragedy of 1941; nor had his knowledge of primary production processes stood him in much stead since.

Next, Martin Wetherall. Unlike James, Martin had taken a First at his university, and followed it up with a brilliant treatise on nuclear fission in the lesser molluscs. It was, then, inevitable that the exigencies of war should demand his presence in Singapore at the crucial moment, together with a party of fellow scientists all sent out at Government expense to study the effects of submarine blast on embryonic barnacle-geese.

Then Penelope Bosworth. Penelope was the eldest of the seven daughters of the Earl of Starveleigh. No one could say that she hadn't been given a fair chance. She had had her London season, her year in India, her six months in Cairo and Pekin; but though her disposition was charming, her mousy appearance, exiguous wardrobe, and lack of any dowry, had so far failed to achieve results. Indeed, had it not been for the war, she would long since have been called home from the East to make way for her second sister Esmé.

Ughtred Thicknesse was descended from a cadet branch of the great Thicknesse family of Thorpnesse-in-Holdernesse. The power and plenty that had accrued to the family under the patronage of Ethelred and, later, Edward the Confessor, had long since been dissipated, and Ughtred, after a lifetime of devoted service in Passport Control, had come to Singapore for his last post, being only three months from his retirement date when the avalanche overtook him.

None of them, even after five years on the island, knew anything of the background of Janice Brown. She was very blonde and very beautiful, and chance remarks she let fall seemed to indicate that at the time of the débâcle she had been staying at Raffles Hotel in a double room.

*   *   *

And now, in August, 1945, they sat together in the stranded launch, to hear on its radio set the General Election results. Penelope and Martin sat together on one side and Janice and Ughtred on the other. James had long been used to this arrangement and sulkily took up his accustomed position in the little cabin, ready to twirl the knobs.

"Don't turn it on till the eleven o'clock news," Janice called out. "I can't imagine anything more boring than long lists of names of people one doesn't know."

Ughtred remarked gently: "One will probably know something of their families even if one doesn't know them personally. Surely we would all find it inspiring to hear that long, slow roll-call of England's greatest, oldest names."

"Well, I wouldn't," Martin said curtly, "I like bad news broken in one short, sharp burst. What do you say, Penelope?"

Penelope looked quickly from one to the other. Two of them said wait, one had said, turn on now; "I think it would be nice to wait," she offered, and Ughtred, knowing her difficulties in offering an opinion, said kindly, "Good news can always wait, can't it?"

James said nothing, sitting gloomily by the radio in the dark. It was always the way — it always *had* been the way, he reflected drearily — no one had ever given him or his opinions the deference due to his social position. Ever since he'd left Oxford and started his enforced tour of the outposts of Empire, rude Colonials had everywhere failed to appreciate that they were being confronted with that perfect flowering of the class system, an English gentleman. But always, in each fresh outpost, James had gone on hoping for a new beginning, for that recognition of his superiority to which he felt his birth and upbringing entitled him. Thus, when they had first come to the island, he had assumed that he would control the situation. He was the only public-school man there — except, of course, for Ughtred, who must be sixty if he was a day, and much too gentle to control anything. The women would, he had assumed, wait on his pleasure, Penelope

to talk of deb dances and Commem balls in the day-
time and Janice — but it hadn't worked out like that.
Penelope and Martin had sat hand in hand from the
start, gone for long walks in the woods collecting
butterflies, and saved each other the best titbits out of
the tins. While as for Janice — there was nothing but
humiliation in the thought of Janice.

She looked such hot stuff, too, he remembered
morosely. Looked as if she couldn't exist if she didn't
have a man in her bed, and he'd thought this was his
chance, his chance to have this blonde smooth woman
with the diamond bracelets, this type of bitch he'd
always longed for and could never afford. But she'd
said, "You don't really love me, do you? It's only my
body you want. I'm not that sort of woman," just as
so many of the women he had ardently desired elsewhere had said to him before. But he'd always noticed
that they only put on this morality act for men without
money; if I was a war profiteer with diamond studs, he
thought bitterly, there'd be none of this blurb about
love. But it riled him intolerably that all this time on
the island Janice never seemed to want to get into bed
with anyone at all, just sat happily by Ughtred's side
and listened entranced while he talked of Edwardian
life in great English country houses.

Damn them all to hell, he thought, they're rotten,
all of them. Wouldn't salute the flag at nightfall,
wouldn't stand to attention when the King made his
speech. But things will be different now. Once we get

rid of this namby-pamby Coalition and have a sound Tory Government with Churchill at the helm. He turned on the wireless.

＊　　　＊　　　＊

Janice said, "They wouldn't nationalize Claridges, would they?"

No one answered. Ughtred said, as if to comfort himself, "After all, they may be Socialists, but they're Britishers. That's what we must cling to — they're Britishers."

"You're pleased, Martin darling, aren't you?" Penelope asked timidly.

Martin said vehemently, "I'm so delighted I can't begin to express it. Do any of you realize what this means? Government of the intellectuals, by the intellectuals, for the intellectuals! That this should have come in my lifetime! God, I'd like to be there to see it."

"Personally," James said, emerging from the cabin, "I don't care if I never see England again now. What I'd like is to go to some wide open space, and make a new life there."

"But, darling," Janice said, "we're in a wide open space with a new life right here and now."

James explained coldly, "I meant somewhere like Rhodesia where caste still has some meaning. Anyway, it's no good shaking the dust of England off my feet if I haven't got it on to shake. If only we could get into touch with the outside world and get someone to take us off this benighted island."

"Oh, we could quite easily, you know," Martin said, standing up. "Come on Penelope, let's go moth-hunting."

"Here," James shouted. "You come back. What the hell do you mean, we could easily get into touch with the outer world?"

"Why, by turning the radio set into a transmitter, of course," Martin explained. "Perfectly simple, if you know how. Come on, Penny."

"But, my dear Martin," Ughtred expostulated, "this is really a matter of some importance. Do you mean to say that all the years we have been on this island you have known that we could, by the exercise of ingenuity, have a wireless transmitter to hand?"

"Of course," Martin said impatiently. "It was perfectly obvious."

"Then why," asked Ughtred, "didn't you mention it?"

"Never thought to," Martin said casually. "Radio's not my subject. What should I do with a wireless transmitter? I can do at least five years more research here on that new variety of *Hippocampus* I discovered last week."

"But, darling," Janice said, tugging at his sleeve, "darling Martin, could *you* turn our radio set into a transmitter?"

"I imagine so," Martin said airily. "If I put my mind to it that is. Perfectly simple application of scientific principles."

"Then you bloody well put your mind to it," James suddenly shouted.

"Look here, I'm not going to be bullied," Martin said querulously. "I've got my own work to do. Just because you've been to Oxford you think you've got the right to order everyone about. We've got a Socialist Government now, and I'm going moth-hunting."

The moon shone out of the velvet sky onto four faces contorted with frustrated hope. James slowly picked up a spanner and moved up to Martin who already had one leg over the gunwale. James raised his hand to strike, but Ughtred caught his arm.

"No," he whispered, "no, that wouldn't help. Martin," he said in a louder voice, "has it ever occurred to you that all your research here may be quite useless? We are by no means on the only island in this group, and it may well be that even on the next one some other stranded scientist may be exactly duplicating your own studies on the *Hippocampus*."

Martin slowly swung his leg back over the gunwale. "No," he said, "somehow that had never occurred to me. Of course, it's perfectly possible. What an absolutely ghastly idea."

"Of course, it must often happen that two people work quite independently on the same lines," Ughtred pursued. "I suppose in such a case the one who first publishes his results gets the credit for it?"

"Naturally," agreed Martin. "But then this other fellow couldn't publish from a desert island any more than I could."

"Ah," said Ughtred with triumphant cunning. "But suppose the other fellow is even at this moment working on turning a radio set into a wireless transmitter?"

❋   ❋   ❋

They had secretly hoped to be rather a hit on the boat that finally heard their appeals and came to pick them up. But the S.S. *Cathartic* had been picking up stranded British subjects for the past three years and had reduced the situation to a routine; handshake with the Captain, whisky with the First Officer, and the ladies to the most motherly stewardess in case they wanted — as they usually did — to weep on her bosom, while she furtively searched for nits in their hair. "Won't have nits on my boat," said the Captain, who thought of everything; then the whip-round for garments and the ladies' little cries when they were told that clothes were rationed at home. "Break their spirit from the start," said the Captain, "they're much less trouble for the rest of the voyage."

So our party tended still to cling together in a nervous little group; James, it must be admitted, found the atmosphere of the P and O line very reassuring, but still could not overcome his shame at the label of Indigent British Subject that the Captain, with great skill, had metaphorically pinned on them all from the start. "Charity keeps people in their place," said the Captain, and it kept James with his party in the little corner they had made their own in the third-class smoking saloon.

Only Martin and Janice, he noticed as the ship neared England, showed increasing eagerness to arrive. Martin, of course, was agog to publish his results and had, in any case, his lectureship at Birmingham University to return to when he got back. And Janice, once she had discovered that the exercise of technique secured her sufficient invitations to spend as much time as she wanted in the first-class bar, was becoming increasingly reconciled to the prospect of living under a Socialist régime at home: "Human nature doesn't change," she would say, as she caught the eye of the Governor-General on the promenade deck, and what matter that he had come to Government House from a miners' lodge instead of a great house? He was still His Excellency and surrounded by assiduous aides-de-camp who were only too anxious to ask Janice to dance.

Martin, when he remembered, would try to allay Penelope's nervousness at the prospect of seeing her family again. "You mustn't be so scared," he would say, impatiently. "They can't hurt you. You're over age and we'll get married as soon as we can and then you'll never have to worry about money again." And Penelope would say, "I know, darling, and it all sounds too wonderful, but do you really think you'll want me when you get back to Birmingham and see all those clever women again?" And Martin would say, "Of course I will, darling." But James could see that Martin thought himself a devilish quixotic fellow to saddle himself with a stupid girl like Penelope in the brave new world he expected when he arrived. And, thought James, if Martin falls out, there'll be nothing for poor Penelope but that ghastly country house in Shropshire and breeding Angora rabbits. Which is a pity, thought James, because she'd be a really nice-looking girl, if somebody had some money to spend on her, but she's never had a fair chance.

Ughtred, however, was in the saddest straits of all. His minute pension, he confided to James one day, would suffice for no more than a room in a boarding-house in Bloomsbury. "And it's not as if I really liked reading," he said sadly. "I like a gentleman's library as well as the next man, and there's no pleasanter place for a night-cap. But after I've paid for my keep, I'll have no money for any amusements of any sort, and there'll be nothing for it but to go and read in the British Museum day after day. I'm told they keep it very warm, but still, it's not what I looked forward to when I entered the service. I'd have some nice rooms in London, I told myself, and there'd be the Club and invitations for the week-ends, and some decent brandy and cigars. Oh, I looked forward to my retirement from the day I started work, but there's not much to look forward to now. Except, of course," he added gratefully, "that they've raised the Old Age Pension."

James was not imaginative, but he was genuinely sorry for Ughtred. He was sorrier, of course, for himself. Ughtred, at least, had started work in the days when social standing and a timely word from an uncle were sufficient to procure a youth a job. Ughtred, at least, had had those years of looking forward to a rosy future, of planning and dreaming. But no hopes brightened James's path. Under this new régime, jobs would call for qualifications and James could muster none. I can dance, he would tell himself, I can shake a ruddy good cocktail, I can ride a good horse and order a good meal. I know how to dress and I'm a good-looking chap. And where will it get me? he questioned resentfully, and answered, To touting vacuum-cleaners at back doors or maybe being a gigolo in a Butlin camp.

As the *Cathartic* swayed uneasily across the Bay of Biscay, James's resentment grew. It's not fair, he would say bitterly, as he watched Penelope's timid face, it's not fair. People like me and Penelope and Ughtred are the salt of the earth. Everyone in the world knows that except for these damned Socialists at home. No wonder they don't get on with the Russkis and can't get all the cash they want from the Yanks. People like the Russkis and the Yanks like dealing with gentlemen, not with a lot of callow intellectuals and agitators no better than themselves. It's not fair, he'd say, as he watched Ughtred plucking nervously at his tie, it's not fair.

He would sit on a bollard on the meagre allotment of third-class deck in the stern and stare above him to the Socialist Governor-General stretched out in a long deck chair with stewards hovering around to bring him soup for his elevenses and stengahs and pahits whenever he wanted them. I suppose that chap used to read H. G. Wells as a lad, he thought resentfully, and think about a Socialist utopia as a sort of dream that could never come off. And now it's come off. There's not many chaps get a chance to live in their own utopias.

He repeated this to Ughtred who strolled up beside him, sucking an empty pipe. "Yes, he's lucky," Ughtred agreed. "Mind you, I quite see that when he was a child, utopias were all he had to look forward to. It's not unfair; our class was living in a utopia then and he's living in one now."

"It may not seem unfair to you," James said savagely. "You've had it. My generation never did and we haven't even got anything to look forward to."

"No, I see that," Ughtred agreed, "and it's a great pity. Mind you, having something to look back on like I have, is much better than nothing; but I do think that people should have something to look forward to, especially when they're down and out. Otherwise they get bitter, and that's such a pity."

"Well, I wish I could see something not to get bitter and hopeless about," James muttered, still staring at the Governor-General who had just lit a large cigar.

Ughtred asked, "Did you ever read a book called *News from Nowhere?*"

"No, what's it about?" James asked without much interest.

"It's another of those Socialist utopia books," said

Ughtred. "I had to read it as a holiday task when I was about fourteen. It's by a fellow called William Morris — chap who did the wallpapers for my grandmother's drawing-room."

"An interior decorator," said James disgustedly.

"Yes, I suppose he must have been," Ughtred agreed, "which would explain why he laid such stress on furnishing fabrics in his utopia. As a matter of fact, that was one of the things that turned me against socialism, when I discovered that it meant that you had to dress in hand-woven materials. I had an aunt who used to weave materials," continued Ughtred reminiscently, "and though she wasn't a Socialist — indeed, very far from it — the idea of wearing her handicraft filled my flesh with abhorrence. Mind you, I have an exceptionally sensitive skin."

"What's all this got to do with looking forward?" asked James.

"Looking forward?" repeated Ughtred. "Ah, I fear I wandered a little away from the point. Reading this book which, as I say, filled me personally with abhorrence, since I dislike few things more than hand-woven fabrics and communal meals, I could yet understand the appeal it might have to those wearing tawdry materials and without enough to eat. I could well understand that to such people hand-woven fabrics and communal meals might represent a utopia to attain which all their energies would be bent. It seems to me, therefore, that it is a great great pity that no analogous book exists to inspire the youth of our own class, a Conservative utopia that might serve to counteract these Socialist dreams."

"Sort of Tory Heaven," commented James with a wry grin.

"Exactly that," said Ughtred, "some rosy account of the goal to which we Conservatives could, if given what is, I believe, called an overwhelming popular mandate, bend our endeavours."

He sighed, and then turned away to resume his daily constitutional in that limited portion of deck allotted to third-class passengers. But James did not notice his going, for he was praying.

Oh God, breathed James to himself with a fervour of intensity hitherto absent from any petition he had addressed to the Almighty. God, let it be as it might have been. Alter the clock, fix the election, do it any way you please, but let me see England as it might be if it weren't for these bloody Socialists, let me see the England of all decent Conservatives' dreams.

He raised an anguished face to the heavens and at that moment a loud clap of thunder was heard over his right shoulder. But James had too little profited by a classical education to appreciate so delicate an allusion. Convinced of the hopelessness of his prayer he lowered his eyes, and saw the coast of England creeping out of the mist.

Chapter 2

JAMES STOOD SULLENLY amid a crowd of third-class passengers and watched the excited bustle of arrival, ropes thrown and caught, gangways slid delicately from shore to ship. He had become separated from his companions. They were, he supposed, in their cabins, trying to bundle together the meagre and pitiable possessions they had been tossed by the Castaways Charitable Fund; all, that is to say, except Janice who, even as James raised his eyes to the upper deck, was, on the arm of the Governor-General, moving confidently to a gangway.

Then something seemed to happen. James, watching with jealous intensity, saw the Governor-General falter and come to a stop. He saw the aides-de-camp move forward and press ahead of their superior. He saw Janice, a bewildered expression on her face, standing uncertainly alone as the Governor-General dropped her arm and began slowly and mechanically climbing down the companionway to the lower deck. Then he heard a loud voice shouting, "Gradation A this way. Gradation A off the ship first, please."

The crowds standing round the gangways seemed, while James watched, to disintegrate and re-form like molecules subjected to a chemical process. The Jewess in the mink coat who had been standing, her jewel case in her hand, ready to step first on to the plank, now slid back into the anonymity of the crowd and her place was taken by a lady in a tweed suit, a felt hat and a *crêpe-de-Chine* blouse. The large Lancashire manufacturer was replaced by a little sandy man with a feather-fly stuck into his shabby green hat. The Governor-General had reached the lower deck now and was standing uneasily behind James, shifting from one foot to another.

One of the shore officials came hustling along the third-class deck. "Any Grade A's here?" he was shouting. "Any Grade A's?"

He stopped and looked at James. "You're a Grade A, aren't you?" he asked briskly. "Got your disc?"

James said, "I don't understand. Is this all something new?'

"Ah," said the official. "Easy to see *you've* not been home lately. Never mind. I'll get you fixed up. Public-school man?"

"Yes," said James vaguely feeling that some Socialist impertinence was intended.

"Which one?" said the man suspiciously.

"Charterhouse," James said haughtily, yet a little ashamed that it wasn't Eton.

But the official seemed to be impressed. "Thought you was a Grade A as soon as I looked at you, sir," he remarked. "You just nip along and get off the ship, and when you go through the security check-up, tell them you haven't been graded. Don't bother about your luggage — the stewards will see to that."

James didn't like to say, in the face of such obvious respect, that he hadn't any luggage, so he turned and climbed up the companionway to the first-class deck. Behind him he could still hear the official shouting. "Any Grade A's down here? Any Grade A's?"

What the devil is it all about, wondered James as he stumbled through the waiting crowds, stumbled down the gangplank. Is it some Socialist dodge to conscript public-school men for the mines, he surmised, as he crossed the quay and dutifully presented himself at an opening in the customs-shed marked "Gradation A." Further away he could see other openings with similar notices, but reading "Gradation B," "Gradation C," and so on.

Inside the door he found, instead of the bleak shed he expected, a superbly designed waiting-room. Armchairs covered in plastic fabrics lined the walls, a central table laden with magazines ran down the room, and at one end of it a barman in a white coat was shaking a cocktail behind a small bar. At the other end of the room was a row of little doors, and sitting in the chairs James recognized some of the people he had seen pressing forward to be first off the boat.

A little door at the end of the room opened, and an official put his head through and said, "Next, please." One of the women got up and went through the door which was closed behind her.

The barman came forward with a tray of drinks. "Will you have a cocktail, sir?" he said to James, who blushed and muttered, "No thanks," furiously resenting his penniless state.

The barman seemed to understand his confusion. "With the compliments of the Southern Railway," he added as if James hadn't spoken. "Dry or sweet, sir? Or would you prefer a pink gin?"

James took a dry Martini, wondering, as he did so, what kind of trick this was. But a free drink's a free drink, he said to himself as he sipped it and watched the little doors at the end opening and closing as more and more passengers were passed through.

At last came the moment when "Next, please," meant that it was James's turn. He gulped down the dregs of his drink, squared his shoulders, and marched grimly in to whatever might face him.

❀   ❀   ❀

"Do please sit down, sir," urged the courteous official who received James in his little office. "I think you'll find that arm-chair perfectly comfortable."

But James remained standing. He burst out, "Look here, what sort of Socialist tomfoolery is this?"

"Socialist?" echoed the official. "Socialist?" and then, "Ah, I understand, sir. You'll be one of the repatriated gentlemen, no doubt. There's been some confusion about them before."

"I don't understand," exclaimed James furiously. "I simply don't understand. What the hell does your Socialist Government — "

The official broke in: "But you see, sir," he said, "we haven't got a Socialist Government."

Shock and bewilderment forced James into the ready armchair. He said weakly: "But the wireless — "

"There's been a lot of misunderstanding," said the official soothingly. "I wouldn't worry your head about it, sir. You just take it from me that we haven't got a Socialist Government, and then, sir, if you wouldn't mind answering some questions — ?"

James was too confused to protest further. Automatically he made his replies to the questions the official read out from the printed form he was holding. Did James play cricket? Had he any titled connections? What were the addresses of his nearest relatives? Had his mother been presented at Court? Some of the questions seemed to James extremely peculiar and he even wondered vaguely whether the official was a crypto-Mass-Observationist, making the most of his opportunities. Still, he owned dutifully to his mother's presentation and his uncle's baronetcy, his standing at school cricket and the family home at Hindhead, and also to a great many other curious details. At the end, the official said, "Well, there seems to be no doubt about your status, sir. If you'll just sign this form, I'll be making you out a temporary gradation disc. They'll let you have your permanent gold disc at headquarters."

James took the form and signed at the foot, noticing, as he did so, that it was headed "Preliminary Social Grading." The official then handed James a duplicate of the form and a small cardboard disc, on which was stamped a large blue A and, in smaller letters, "Ministry of Social Security."

"When you get to London, you just call on the Ministry's office in Curzon Street and they'll fix you up with everything," said the official. He coughed discreetly. "There's just one more small point, sir, if I may make so bold as to mention it." He coughed discreetly. "How are you fixed for cash, sir?"

James to his horror felt himself blushing and then blushed still redder with fury. The official seemed to understand his confusion and, fumbling inside a drawer, produced a little bag which he held out to James. "There are twenty gold sovereigns here, sir," he said. "If you'll just sign this receipt?" He held out a pen.

"But look here — "spluttered James. He felt alarmed. Was the man mad? "What would I do with gold sovereigns? — and anyway how should I ever pay it back?"

"All Grade A's use gold sovereigns," said the official firmly. "And as for paying it back — well, the usual thing is for headquarters to deduct it from your income."

James wanted to protest that he hadn't got an income, but the whole situation seemed to be getting beyond him. Weakly he took the bag, signed the receipt, and then said, "Is that all?"

"Not quite," said the official smoothly. "Here is your train ticket — I take it that you are going to London?"

"Might as well," muttered James.

"I would certainly advise you to go to headquarters as soon as possible," urged the official. James took the tickets, stuffed them into his pocket and began to make for the door.

"This way, if you please," said the official, indicating a door at the other side that had escaped James's notice. He held it open politely, and James said awkwardly, "Oh, sorry," and turned to pass through. The official caught at his sleeve.

"Excuse me, sir," he whispered hoarsely. "You fixed up for a hotel in London?"

James shook his head. He felt a card thrust into his hand. "You take my advice," whispered the official. "It's a very good hotel. Special arrangements, sir, for gentlemen travelling alone." James was astonished to notice that one official eye closed in a large bland wink.

"That will be all, I think, sir," pursued the official, using his normal official voice again. "Good-day, sir," and James was bowed out.

*   *   *

He found himself on the platform, facing a train entirely composed of Pullman cars, the familiar little pink-shaded lamps winking from their windows. "Not much austerity about that," said James to himself, for it must be remembered that James, together with the rest of his party, had steadily followed on the wireless what they imagined to be the contemporary news from England. Now he pulled from his pocket the tickets he had been given. "Car B, seat 7" he read, and sure enough, facing him, stood Car B, the name *Corybante* neatly picked out in letters of gold along its flank.

But James did not immediately mount, for suddenly it occurred to him to wonder what had become of his companions. Had they, too, been through these peculiar formalities and been presented with bags of gold similar to the one that even now was weighing down the right-hand pocket of the rather inferior trousers presented to him by the Castaways' Charitable Association? He stood still and looked about him.

More and more people were emerging from the little official doors and climbing onto the train, but he could not, for the moment, see any of his former companions. "All aboard," shouted the guard, and James couldn't hesitate any longer. He jumped on to the step of his car and, as the train gave its preliminary snorts, took a last look about him.

Stay! Surely that was Martin, tramping along the platform, his shoulders hunched, his bag dragging heavily in his hand, his eyes fixed on the ground. "Martin!" shouted James excitedly, momentarily forgetting old enmities in relief at the sight of a familiar face, "Martin, here!" Martin started, stopped in his hunching tramp, and looked up at James, poised on the step of the Pullman car. On his face was such an expression of bewilderment, disappointment and defeat, that James was shocked and speechless. Then Martin lowered his eyes to the ground again, the train gathered speed, and there was nothing for James to do but retreat into the Pullman car and pull the door shut behind him.

＊　　　＊　　　＊

The train was hurrying now through the suburbs of Southampton. James stumbled along the swaying car and found seat 7, and lowered himself into it. Opposite him was the little sandy man whom James had noticed taking precedence off the ship. He, lowering his *Times*, met James's eye and barked, "Jolly to be back in England, what?"

"I'm not so sure yet," said James cautiously.

"Nonsense," said the little man. "Nonsense. I know what it is — you need a drink." He pressed a bell, and an obsequious waiter stood beside the table. "Two double whiskies and quick," said the little man peremptorily, and the waiter scuttled off.

"Very good of you," said James and couldn't help adding, "But isn't it outside hours?"

"Nonsense, nonsense," said the little man sharply. "No licensing hours for Grade A's. Easy to see you've been out of England, my boy." The attendant brought the drinks, and James was interested to note that the little man fished a gold sovereign out of his pocket and proffered it to the waiter, who accepted it without comment, handing back what seemed to be a gold half-sovereign together with silver.

"Here's how," said the little man, and James repeated "Here's how," as they both raised their glasses and drank.

The little man heaved a contented sigh. "The first English whisky always tastes pretty good, eh?" he said. "Somehow whisky never tastes the same in India."

"You're from India, are you?" commented James politely.

"Yes, indeed," said the little man, "and in one of the best jobs in the world."

"Oh," said James without much interest, "and what is that?"

"Empire-building," said the little man vehemently and smacked his glass down on the table.

"But surely," ventured James diffidently, "Empire-building in India must be pretty well finished, as jobs go?"

"But it's only just beginning!" protested the little man in apparent amazement, and then, "Oh, I see. You've not been back in England since the new régime took over?" James shook his head. "Well, then, you take it from me, young man, India under present-day conditions offers the greatest possible opportunities for men of vigour, stamina, initiative and — er — presence." He looked modestly down his nose,

"And what," asked James, feeling his way, "are present-day conditions in India?"

"Not much good at history," barked the little man. "By the way, my name's Hardiman — but I suppose I'd better explain as best I can."

"Please do," begged James, feeling that perhaps some light might now be cast on the penumbra of confusion that had surrounded him since the *Cathartic* tied up.

"Well," said Mr. Hardiman, "things started to change as soon as the new régime took over. Once the niggers saw that it was a question of dealing with gentlemen, their whole attitude changed. They all got together — Hindus, Moslems, Princes and all — and begged the English to come back. 'We're used to dealing with Sahibs,' they said, 'and we like it.' Well, we couldn't refuse. And after the Royal Visit went off last summer, there hasn't been a loyaller, more contented jewel in the Imperial crown." He drained his whisky, murmuring as he did so, "The King-Emperor, God bless him."

Mr. Hardiman picked up his *Times* and once more ensconced himself behind it, leaving James to a medley of conflicting thoughts. What the devil, what the devil, he wondered, had happened to England? Surely it was only this morning that he had been sitting moodily on a bollard on the third-class deck of the *Cathartic* watching Janice dallying above him with the Socialist Governor-General? Certainly socialism had then seemed rampant and well on the up and up. And now? The one thing everyone had seemed anxious to assure him since was that whatever kind of government England now had, it wasn't a Socialist one. James wished passionately that he had thought to buy a paper at Southampton. He tried to peer at Mr. Hardiman's, but *The Times,* as always, presented unhelpful back and front pages to his avid glance. He looked round the compartment, but there was no help there. Groups of palpably British ladies and gentlemen sat around their respective tables and chatted in loud and well-bred voices. James heard, " — so I wrote to Marshall and Snelgrove, and they sent the very thing by the next airmail — " Nothing could have been more ordinary, more normal.

He looked out of the window. It was a fine spring day with puffs of blossoms dotted over a countryside that always seems, whether in prosperity, crisis or catastrophe, more secure, more established, more verdant than any other in the world. James swept it with a questing critical eye, but he could not find that it looked other than usual. There was no help there. He leant back in his plush seat and closed his bewildered eyes.

*　　　*　　　*

When he opened them again, the train was running through the southern suburbs of London. Opposite him, Mr. Hardiman was snoring gently, his *Times* lying limp on his lap. But James had no eyes for it now, for he was staring out of the window, eager to see his first sight of the bomb damage of which the wireless had given such graphic descriptions.

Yes, it was all there; the church that was no more than an empty shell, the blackened girders of a burnt-out factory, the ineffectual fireplaces poised on the walls of devastated dwellings. He saw, too, little colonies of square white boxes like children's toys that he knew must be the prefabricated dwellings of which he had heard tell. The train began to slacken speed and James saw the towers of the Battersea Power Station belching their clean white smoke over London. "Never did like that building," he reflected, "much too gaunt. Couldn't see why people made such a fuss about it." The train slid decorously into Waterloo station.

The Pullman-car attendant called out: "If passengers will kindly keep their seats, the porters will board the train and receive their instructions." And sure enough, a file of porters immediately appeared, each one attaching himself to one of the groups in the saloon.

One stopped in front of Mr. Hardiman and James and courteously asked, "Are you two gentlemen together?"

"No," replied Mr. Hardiman, "we are not, but perhaps," he added, turning to James, "if you are going in the same direction, we might share a taxi?"

"Well, I'm not quite sure which direction I *am* going in," said James awkwardly, fumbling in his pocket. He pulled out the card the official gave him. "I was recommended to this place by the official at Southampton," he said. "I don't know if it's any good?"

Mr. Hardimen adjusted his glasses and leant forward to read "THE CONINGSBY HOTEL, ST. JAMES SQUARE, S.W." "You couldn't do better," he said cordially. "I'd go there myself, only I've got my sister expecting me in

Kensington. Well, we both go in the same way. You just got the one bag? I sent my heavy luggage ahead, too, so we might as well be off."

The porter picked up the two bags and then stood aside to let his gentlemen off the train. James was delighted to see a row of taxis immediately opposite and that there was none of that queueing he had been led to expect. The porter, having darted ahead, had already placed their bags inside one of them and was holding its door invitingly open. James gave the address of the Coningsby Hotel, and the gentlemen climbed in. The porter shut the door and away they went.

Up Buckingham Palace Road, past the Palace, through St. James's Park. The brightly planted flower beds glittered gaily in the sunshine and the sentries outside the Palace had resumed, James was glad to see, their bearskins and scarlet coats. He said as much to Mr. Hardiman who commented, "Yes, indeed, very proper. Delighted to see it," and the taxi sped on.

It stopped in a little cul-de-sac off St. James's Street before a low Georgian house with flower boxes at its window sills. Hardly had it stopped when the door was opened by a liveried flunkey, and a rubicund man with white side whiskers came bustling out, so clearly the "Mine Host" of every Victorian drawing that James who, while knowing what he liked, was not in the least artistic, instantly recognized him as such.

"Why, Mr. Hardiman, you *are* a stranger," now said

Mine Host genially rubbing his hands together, "and are we to have the pleasure of your company again?"

"I fear not, Harbottle, I fear not," responded Mr. Hardiman, "no, it is my young friend here who has come to sample the delights of your excellent hostelry. Let me recommend him to your attention."

"Any friend of yours, Mr. Hardiman, any friend of yours," said Mine Host, standing aside to let James get out of the taxi.

"Good-bye," he said to Mr. Hardiman, and Mr. Hardiman said cordially, "I hope we shall meet again. I should be interested to hear your impressions of our new England." The flunkey gently closed the taxi door and James preceded Mine Host into the hotel.

❊   ❊   ❊

Its outward appearance was belied by an entrance hall of most inviting Tudor aspect. Its walls were properly panelled in dark oak and decorated with hunting-prints of elongated horses and attenuated huntsmen; a log fire burnt brightly in an open hearth; chintz-covered sofas and armchairs stood about the room, many of them filled by hatchet-faced men in tweeds or well-cut lounge suits with those bronzed visages that betoken a sufficiency of leisure passed in the open air.

Harbottle led James past these to a little glassed-in office. "Now if you'll just let me see your disc, sir," he said genially, "and then sign the visitors' book — "

Disc, thought James wildly, disc — ? Harbottle perceived his confusion.

"I take it you've just landed in England, sir," he said, as so many other people had said to James today. "I mean the disc they handed you at the Immigration Office, sir."

James suddenly remembered the little circle of cardboard handed to him by the official. He now fished this out of his pocket and handed it to Harbottle, who took a cursory glance at it and murmured deprecatingly: "Merely a formality, sir, as I'm sure you understand," as he pushed the visitors' book towards James.

James duly signed and handed the pen back to Harbottle who now coughed discreetly as he said with meaning: "I take it, sir, that you will be requiring All Amenities."

"I should just think so," said James vehemently, patting the gold in his trouser pocket and thinking longingly of soft beds and bacon and clean shoes and one and another such thing.

"Then that will be perfectly all right, sir," said Mr. Harbottle and rang a bell on his desk, at which a flunkey appeared who was told to take Mr. Leigh-Smith up to number 27.

This menial led James through a series of corridors so pleasingly tortuous and irregular that one was forced to believe that the building had been given either a newer exterior or an older inside. At last they came to number 27.

His bedroom was, James was pleased to see, furnished in one of the styles he considered most admirable, namely that of the English country house. Some flower prints on the wall, a bright fire in the grate, chintz curtains and bedspread and a modern lavatory basin in one corner — all combined to make James feel at home. "The bathroom is here, sir," said the flunkey flinging open a door in the wall. "We have one for every bedroom in order to comply with the standard laid down by the United States Tourists' Advisory Committee." James looked into the bathroom and saw, as well as the most modern sanitary equipment, a cherry-cheeked maid of extremely delightful appearance laying out some towels. The flunkey closed the bathroom door again, saying, "I trust, sir, that everything is entirely satisfactory." "Entirely," replied James. "The tap-water is filtered," added the flunkey, "and iced water is piped on, but I don't suppose that being an English gentleman, sir, you care about that. Dinner is served in the dining-room at any time you choose, sir. Is there anything else I can do for you?" James took the opportunity of getting the flunkey to change one of his sovereigns for him and then, after rewarding him suitably, let him go.

It must be admitted that James now went straight to the bathroom to see if the cherry-cheeked maid was still there, but she had apparently left by the outer door. So James took a bath, revelling in the hot water, the super-fatted soap and the enormous fleecy towels —

but hadn't he heard, he reflected, that soap and towels were no longer provided by most hotels? Evidently he had struck lucky, and he blessed that official at Southampton.

It was now eight o'clock and James resolved to dine straightaway and then go to bed early in order to be ready for this strange interview he had to have in the morning. Consequently he dressed himself again regretting, as he did so, the unpleasing cut of his charity suit, and descended to the lounge.

A waiter came forward as he hesitated uncertainly at the foot of the stairs. "Would you care for a sherry in the lounge, sir?" he inquired politely, "or would you prefer to go straight in to dinner?" "I think I'll go straight in," said James, and the waiter said, "Certainly, sir. This way, if you please, sir," and led him to the dining-room.

And what a pleasant room it was, thought James, his eye resting with pleasure on the small round tables, each decked in immaculate damask and lit by its own silver candalabrum. He sat down at one of these, noticing with surprise as he did so that the table silver seemed to be genuine, the linen of the finest quality, and the glasses most delicate and fine.

Now a menu was placed before him and he read it with growing incredulity and amazement. Surely this must be a jest? Surely he could not have *foie gras* followed by a grilled sole followed by a roast duck with green peas and finished by strawberries and cream?

He ordered these, and the bottle of Beaune suggested by the wine waiter, with defiance, certain in his own mind that some elaborate joke was being played and that none of these could possibly materialize. But materialize they all did, and so did the coffee and the Armagnac and the Havana that James, with growing excitement, treated himself to afterwards. He sat at the table glowing in a mist of enchantment.

It can't be true, he was telling himself, it can't be true. It's all a dream and soon I shall wake up. It *can't* be true. Abruptly he rose from the table, determined to take a short walk before turning in and try to clear a head that could not, he thought, be other than fuddled, although he knew in his heart that he had never felt better in his life.

In the fine spring evening he walked up St. James's Street towards Piccadilly. It all seemed very much as he had remembered it before the war. Only one change he noticed — the Lyons he remembered on the eastern side of the street was no longer there; a small change, he reflected, after so many years. Apart from that, the same or, it appeared to him, even more expensive cars seemed to be rolling up and down the street and among them, James noticed to his delight, a few hansom cabs. Nor were these, as might have been expected, battered and shabby, but, on the contrary, glistening with fresh paint and polished brass and drawn by well-groomed horses. "I suppose the petrol shortage has brought them out," reflected James, "and very nice, too," for hansom cabs, though he himself was far too young to have known them, roused in him a medley of pleasing associations. He threw away the butt of his cigar and retraced his footsteps to the Coningsby Hotel.

James bade a courteous "good-night" to Harbottle who was hovering in the hall, and went upstairs along the twisting corridors to his room. He unlocked the door and went in.

Judge of his amazement, then, when he saw, as he switched the light on, a female form already in the bed. She turned her face towards him, and he recognized the cherry-cheeked maid he had already admired in the bathroom.

"I say," he stammered. "I say — I mean to say — that is — I think there must be some mistake."

The face in the bed looked distressed. "You *did* ask for All Amenities, didn't you?" it inquired.

James thought back to his conversation with Harbottle. "Er — yes," he replied, "I suppose I did."

"Then *that's* all right," said the cherry-cheeked maid, and flashed a welcoming smile at James. "I go with the bed."

Chapter 3

JAMES woke next morning to find himself sole possessor of his bed. On the whole, he felt rather relieved. Without in any way wishing to decry those pleasures he had lately enjoyed, his present wish was wholly for breakfast and he would have resented anything that might have stood between him and it. "But I rather think I'd better slip down to Sussex tonight and see the old people," he reflected, as he rang for a cup of tea; for James, despite many boasts he had exchanged with his fellows, preferred performance that might be considered moderate but still assured.

Breakfast, he found, when, washed and shaved, he descended to the dining-room, was all that dinner the night before might have led one to expect; on a gigantic mahogany sideboard simmered grilled kidneys and deviled chicken, huge mounds of scrambled eggs, bacon, sausages and even trout. Discarding a proffered roll as having altogether too foreign a look, James surrounded himself with toast, butter, marmalade, honey and coffee, let the waiter help him to a large plate of porridge and prepared to enjoy himself.

"I've eaten pretty well all over the world," he reflected, as he liberally sprinkled his porridge with brown sugar and soused it with thick cream. (James had no such Scottish origins as impelled him to ruin

36

a good dish with salt.) "And in all the world I am quite convinced there isn't a meal to compare with an English breakfast, though I must admit that the coffee isn't usually all it might be." Here he nodded to the waiter to fill up his cup and then sipped the brew gingerly. His worst fears were realized; the coffee was as appalling as ever.

The waiter, however, who was hovering solicitously by, noticed his wry face, and with a deft gesture whisked away his cup. "I *beg* your pardon, sir," he said, "most of our gentlemen prefer the English brew, sir, but for travelled gentlemen we always keep a special pot." He disappeared and came back with a fresh cup of coffee which James, upon examination, found to be as delicious as any he had ever tasted anywhere in the world.

Up till now, James had accepted the many strange incidents that had befallen him with, it is true, a great deal of bewilderment, but without any fundamental desire to find out what it was all about; he had simply remained passive and let things happen to him.

It was only now, drinking his cup of excellent coffee, that James finally realized that in some queer way England was radically changed. You may think him singularly unperspicacious not to have realized this before, but it was the very nature of the change that befogged him. In some peculiar way this new England seemed — not strange, but wholly familiar to him, like a dream so persistent in his subconscious that he welcomed it as a part of himself.

"But I really must find out what it's all about," he mused as he entered upon two fried eggs with tomatoes, chipolatas and bacon. He toyed with the notion of ordering a copy of *The Times,* as had so many of the gentlemen breakfasting around him, but decided against. "It's a deuced difficult paper to read," he said to himself, "and half the time you're no wiser than when you started." He would really have liked a *Daily Mirror* to see in what *milieu* Jane was at present undressed, but was nervous of asking for it in these surroundings. "The best thing I can do," he resolved, "is to cut along and see these Ministry types as soon as I can."

So he finished his breakfast with immense enjoyment and soon afterwards was ready to walk to Curzon Street. It was a perfect spring day. Little white clouds puffed across the pale blue sky and the Portland stone of the buildings was lit with its peculiar and mellow summer glow. Walking up St. James's Street, James marvelled at the numbers of well-dressed women and well-groomed men that passed him. There was none of that shabby tired flurry that he had been told was the aftermath of metropolitan war. Instead, with an appearance of perfect breeding and leisure, ladies and gentlemen strolled up and down St. James's Street, and in the window of Boodles, loungers screwed their eyeglasses into their eyes and gazed at the scene with every evidence of pride and enjoyment.

So James came to Piccadilly and here a more animated

scene met his eye. The crowds who thronged the street seemed altogether more mixed, and James, who after his island seclusion was still unused to crowds, crossed Piccadilly as soon as he could and prepared to slip into Albemarle Street, which looked to him surprisingly empty.

He was soon to learn the reason. As he came to the corner he saw what had earlier escaped his eye, that the road was barred with a large white wooden gate, such as one finds on many a country estate. On it was hung a placard that read, in admirably placed Roman capitals:

THE MAYFAIR ESTATE
PRIVATE
ADMITTANCE BY DISC

and beside the gate, apparently its guardian, stood a man in dark blue livery with a cockaded hat.

James was so nonplussed by this unexpected apparition that he did not behave with the tact we should like to expect of him. He marched straight up to the gatekeeper and said: "Open that thing, I want to get through."

The countenance of the gatekeeper, which had hitherto been imbued with that insolent nonchalance characteristic of good servants, now changed. He looked sneeringly at James's improperly shabby suit and jeered, "And who d'you think *you* are, eh? Lord High Muck? Can't you read?" and he jerked his finger to the notice beside him.

James quivered with indignation and said with immense passion, "Let me through, I tell you. I have an appointment with some Ministry in Curzon Street. Let me through at once."

"That be buggered for a story," said the gatekeeper, and spat in the road, "not much use your coming that one in a suit like that. The Curzon Street branch only deals with A's."

"But I am an A, damn you!" said James suddenly comprehending the last line of the poster, and he pulled out his cardboard disc and thrust it into the gatekeeper's face.

The gatekeeper's whole demeanour instantaneously and ludicrously changed. With shaking hands he unlocked the gate and then, apparently too aghast for words, stood aside to let James pass through.

James pursued his way with a sense of jubilation. There are few things more pleasant than admission to any area from which the general public is debarred and James felt immensely though irrationally proud of himself. "That little circle of cardboard certainly seems to have what it takes," he reflected complacently, and strode jubilantly on towards his destination.

*　　　*　　　*

James noticed, as he walked, that altogether herculean efforts seemed to have been made to restore Mayfair to something not merely approaching but even surpassing its pre-war splendour. In Berkeley Square many of the houses were gay with window boxes, and the gardens in the centre were verdant with lawns and trees under which played clearly superior children. Nowhere was there any sign of bomb damage; everywhere was redolent of peace and prosperity.

At the corner of Curzon Street James hesitated and finally asked a convenient policeman which way he should turn for the Ministry. "You mean the Ministry of Social Security?" inquired the policeman, and then directed James to an impressive mansion close to the Curzon Cinema.

Had it not been for the policeman's help, James might easily have passed it by, for only a discreet brass plate inside the beautiful Queen Anne porch proclaimed its identity. James marched boldly up the steps and then found to his surprise that the front door was firmly shut. "But they told me to come this morning," he argued to himself. "No one said it was a holiday or anything," and tentatively he pressed the bell beside the door.

It was immediately opened by an impressive butler who bowed politely to James and then waited for him to speak. But James was momentarily at a loss for words. Surely he must have come to the wrong place? At last he managed to stammer out, "I'm looking for the Ministry of Social Security."

"Yes, sir," said the butler, "and whom did you wish to see?"

"Well, I wouldn't know about that," said James. "I

was told to come here by some official at Southampton."

"Oh, yes, sir," said the butler with apparent comprehension and asked James his name. Then, "If you'll just come this way, sir," he said. He led James through a magnificent vestibule, through a vast mahogany door, into a comfortable waiting-room, plentifully bestrewed, as James saw at first glance, with *Punches* and *Tatlers* along an immense mahogany table. By the window, a man with his back to James was just picking up his hat and stick, apparently preparatory to leaving. He turned and James saw his face.

"Ughtred!" he cried gladly, and flung himself upon him, ecstatically shaking his hand.

"Well, James, this *is* really very nice," commented Ughtred with his habitual friendly calm. "Do you know, you are the first of our island companions that I have seen since we left the ship."

"I haven't seen anyone either," responded James. "By Jove, it *is* good to see you again." Indeed it was only now, in the excitement of seeing Ughtred, that he realized just how very lost and lonely he had felt in this new and incomprehensible London.

The door opened and the massive butler reappeared. "Mr. Leigh-Smith," he trumpeted, "Mr. Featherstone-haugh will see you now, sir."

"Ughtred," James said urgently, "Wait for me, won't you? There's so much I want to talk to you about."

"I will gladly wait for you, James," Ughtred replied, settling himself in one of the mahogany chairs and picking up a *Punch.* "Perhaps, when you're through with your business, you would like to come along to my club, and we could have our chat over some of our excellent old sherry."

"Your club!" James exclaimed in surprise, remembering how Ughtred had told him that the expense of a club subscription would be far beyond his means. He fixed incredulous eyes on Ughtred who, under his gaze, slowly turned deep crimson from his forehead to his collar. The butler was still waiting in the doorway. "Don't suppose I'll be long," James said, and he squared his shoulders and walked to the door.

❀   ❀   ❀

On his way up the great carved marble staircase, James decided that he would not try to find out here what the whole bewildering confusion was about. For one thing, he disliked the idea of being beholden to a Government official for anything. For another, he had become so accustomed, during the past years, to ask Ughtred for information on all subjects, that he preferred to wait until he could question this mentor again. On principle, James disliked asking for information, holding that a sensible man could, if he kept his eyes and ears open, easily discover all that it was useful to him to know. But if he *had* to know about something beyond his own experience — well, then, Ughtred was the man to ask. Without being in any way one of those didactic intellectuals — and here James always thought distastefully of Martin — Ughtred was still James's idea of an educated English gentleman, which meant that he could discourse pleasantly on any decent subject without knowing enough to become boring about any of them. Yes, decidedly he would wait and ask Ughtred.

*   *   *

Mr. Featherstonehaugh advanced from behind his Sheraton desk to welcome James. "My dear fellow," he said, shaking his hand, "how very much relieved you must be to have reached England again after your war-time vicissitudes."

"Not sure about that yet," said James cautiously. He didn't much care for these effusive chaps, not in offices, anyway, when none of that charm of manner could possibly lead up to a drink. But Mr. Featherstonehaugh was saying: "Now what can I offer you? We've got some Scotch here we're really proud of," and, taking James's surprised start for a nod of assent, Mr. Featherstonehaugh turned to a handsome cabinet and started to pour whisky into carved Jacobean glasses.

Not even backview did James really like the look of Mr. Featherstonehaugh. "All that Eton manner," he growled to himself, "and what the devil does the fellow want to wear a butterfly collar and side whiskers for, he can't be more than my age and he looks like a Victorian statesman." But even James's resentment began to melt when he found himself sitting in a comfortable wing chair and sipping the Scotch of which Mr. Featherstonehaugh was justly proud.

"And now," said Mr. Featherstonehaugh, "to business." He picked up a paper from his desk. "I have here the dossier you filled in at Southampton," he continued, "and really, it is so impeccable that we don't feel it necessary to question you farther on it." He scanned it rapidly. "Most satisfactory, most satisfactory," he murmured, half to himself. "The very type the new régime is so *very* instrumental in saving." He took a swig at his whisky, and went on in a louder voice, "It only remains, then, Mr. Leigh-Smith, for me to find out what your plans are and see what we can do to assist you to realize them."

"That's very kind of you," said James, a little uncomfortably. "But to tell you the truth, I haven't really got any plans yet. Except that I'd vaguely thought of emigrating."

"Oh, come, Mr. Leigh-Smith," said Mr. Featherstonehaugh protestingly, "I can hardly feel that you will want to do that when you've seen a little more of England." He leant over the table and said confidentially, "Now tell me, honestly, what would you most *like* to be able to do?"

To his surprise James heard himself saying, "I'd like to be a Man-About-Town."

Mr. Featherstonehaugh leapt to his feet, his face transfigured with joy. "Mr. Leigh-Smith," he breathed in an awe-struck whisper, "Mr. Leigh-Smith, do you really mean that?"

"Well — er — I mean — " mumbled James, and then, belligerently, "Yes, I do mean it. You asked me, didn't you, and now you've got it. If I could really choose, that's what I'd like to be."

Mr. Featherstonehaugh had seized James's hand and seemed to be shaking it as vigorously as his somewhat etiolated frame would allow. "Mr. Leigh-Smith," he said, "I'm delighted, absolutely delighted. I think you have made a very courageous decision."

"Well — " began James confusedly, but Mr. Featherstonehaugh was in full spate.

"You wouldn't believe," he was saying, "you wouldn't believe, my dear Mr. Leigh-Smith, the difficulty we have had in inducing our youth to take to this particular career. You'd think that the advantages were obvious — after all, Men-About-Town are really the cream of a society such as ours — but no! the memory of the bad old days seemed to have entered into their blood. They were always afraid that times might change, that they might be left high and dry, forgotten by the community without a word of thanks. One tries to explain that society has need of them, but — well, I sometimes think that *courage* is what is lacking." He shook his head sadly, and looked down into his whisky. James, who hadn't made head or tail of what he was saying, looked awkwardly away.

"Come, come," said Mr. Featherstonehaugh, seemingly brightening, "I mustn't burden you with our troubles, particularly when you have just made the very decision that we are asking for. What we must do is to get *you* fixed up as quickly as possible." He rummaged among the papers on his desk and finally selected a long pink form. "About finance," he said, his pen poised above it.

"Yes?" commented James with interest.

"*About* three thousand a year, I should say," murmured Mr. Featherstonehaugh. "Any particular interest? — oh, yes, I remember now — " he pulled James's dossier towards him, "Oh, yes — coffee, rubber, nitrates — " he now consulted a sort of paper-bound directory that stood near his hand, and then started scribbling on the pink form. At last, "I think I've got three excellent directorships for you," he said, looking up. "M'bwanga Rubber, Associated Nitrates, and White Kenya Coffee Company. All most admirable firms. The actual fees, of course, are negligible — I think we can disregard them — but the expense accounts, of course, are the thing. I was lucky to get M'bwanga for you; it's one of the few carrying a straight two thousand a year. Nitrates and White Kenya are each worth five hundred to you, but they're both going up in the world and I shouldn't be a bit surprised to see the expense accounts raised quite a bit by this time next year. Pity about the director's fees, though." He sighed.

"Why?" asked James.

"Well," explained Mr. Featherstonehaugh, with evident embarrassment, "the fact of the matter is, they're subject to Income Tax." He looked uneasily at James, and then threw down his pen. "I know what you're thinking," he said protestingly, "but we couldn't help it. We *couldn't* do everything at once. Something had to be subject to Income Tax, just for the sake of appearance. But you'll come out all right on three thousand, won't you?" he added pleadingly.

"I should just about think so," maintained James with feeling.

Mr. Featherstonehaugh picked up his pen again. "Now will you be actually wanting a post with an office? Oh, no," he interjected, "I see you're not married yet. Married men usually like to have an office to go to. By the way, do you want us to see about getting you a wife?"

James said forcibly, "Certainly not."

Mr. Featherstonehaugh didn't seem at all put out by his manner. "Oh, all right," he said nonchalantly. "Just let us know if you do, that's all. Our lists are most complete, and it's a convenience to have us fix all the dowry business for you. Now, what next? A club, of course. What do you think of the Outlanders? It's very well thought of by young men like yourself who have travelled a bit."

"All right," James amiably agreed.

"And then," said Mr. Featherstonehaugh, "a tailor." He consulted another list. Yes, Spits and Pluckem have a vacancy — a very good firm." He beamed at James. 'Now, have you thought where you're going to live?"

"Not yet," James said. "I haven't really had a chance."

Mr. Featherstonehaugh was clearly getting into his stride. "I can fix you up with some very nice little chambers in St. James's," he offered, "run by a really admirable ex-butler and his wife who is, I understand, a first-class cook. They used to belong to the Honourable William ffitz-Slough, but we arranged him a very good marriage so now he's in Grosvenor Square. How do you think that would do?"

"Nicely, I should think," said James, still determined not to comment on this farrago of incomprehensibility.

"Then that, I think, will be all," concluded Mr. Featherstonehaugh. He handed James a card. "Here is your new address," he said. "I will send round a list of your accounts at the various shops, and will see that you get some cards from dinner hostesses to put on your mantelpiece. And oh, I nearly forgot." He opened a drawer and pulled out a little morocco box. "Here is your permanent disc — and let me wish you prosperity and happiness under our new régime."

James snapped open the box. On a velvet bed reposed a round gold medal with milled edges. One side was embossed with a dainty design of primroses. The other simply read "James Leigh-Smith."

"Older men often hang them on their watch chains," Mr. Featherstonehaugh commented. "But personally, I had a little gold wristlet made for it. Much more *chic.*" He shook James's hand at the door, and the gold disc dangled below his stiff cuff.

"Ughtred," asked James curiously as he and his old friend left the Ministry together. "What did you decide to be?"

"I?" said Ughtred. "Oh, that was easy. I decided to be a clubman."

Chapter 4

THEY were seated in Ughtred's club in deep brown leather armchairs. The inevitable May chill that permeated the outside air was effectively dispelled by the blazing log and coal fire before which the two gentlemen stretched their legs. Ughtred had rung for sherry and a decanter filled with tawny Amontillado stood on the small table between them. James was smoking a cigarette and Ughtred had just pulled out his pipe. So far, only the most trivial small talk had been exchanged. The room was empty save for an elderly member in a frock coat who snored gently in one corner.

"And now, Ughtred," said James with determination, "please explain."

There was a moment's silence. James, who for the past twenty-four hours had longed for nothing more than to discover what it was all about, now oddly began to wonder if he really wanted to know. Cold facts, thought James (who in common with most of his countrymen never used that noun without the qualifying adjective) can be so chilling — and the present seemed so very, very rosy and warm. Did he really want to know?

But Ughtred had knocked out his pipe on the tall club fender and was beginning to speak.

"It's not," he was saying, "as if I can really give you a full picture. You must remember I've only been in

England as long as you have, and it was only yesterday evening, here in the club, that I began to have some notion what it was all about.

"You will remember that while we were on our little island we had some account of a General Election that the Socialists were said to have won. That, I understand was true. It also appears to be true that the Labour Government embarked on a comprehensive programme of egalitarian rule, thus continuing the levelling process that had begun many years before and noticeably extended during the last war.

"Now it appears that after this process had continued for some little while, a general revulsion against it began to be felt by the entire population. The strange thing seems to have been that this revulsion was for so long totally — or almost totally — disregarded. Public-opinion polls seemed somehow to miss it — true, their results showed increasing dissatisfaction with the Labour Government, but never any wish or enthusiasm to have the Liberals or Conservatives in their stead."

"Why was that?" interpolated James in surprise.

"I gather it was the fault of the Conservatives themselves," replied Ughtred, "they had themselves become so endoctrinated with the Socialist theory that the tentative programme they had finally produced after years of gestation was inevitably based on the principle that all men are created equal. And this was just the very idea that the public had begun fundamentally to reject.

"Only two groups in this country seem to have understood the way the public mind was working. These were — draw your chair a litle closer, James — the Intellectuals — "

"Ughtred, why are you whispering?" asked James in surprise.

Ughtred said, still in the same low voice, "Everyone seems to whisper when they mention the Intellectuals — I think you'll see why in a minute."

"Oh, all right," grunted James. "Who were the other group?"

"The others," continued Ughtred, "were a caucus of extremely retrogressive Conservatives under the leadership of Sir W—— S——."

"Fascists?" queried James.

"Definitely," said Ughtred, sipping his sherry. "No! That's an idea you must get right out of your head. I must admit that that was the first idea that crossed my mind, but I am assured that nothing could be further from the truth. It has long been an article of British faith that fascism is a nasty foreign notion, whereas the anti-egalitarianism I am describing seems to be totally and basically English."

"But what happened?" asked James with interest. "What did the Intellectuals do?"

"Sh — " motioned Ughtred urgently, but already the old gentleman in the corner had stirred uneasily in his sleep. He opened one angry and bleary eye and glanced suspiciously at the room then, seeing nothing apparent to disturb him in the sight of two well-bred gentlemen conversing by the fire, closed it, and started snoring again.

"It seems," whispered Ughtred, "that the Intellectuals, by nasty underhand methods like using their brains, got in first. Under socialism they had already attained key positions in the State; now they suddenly staged a *coup d'état.*"

"Gosh!" gasped James, shocked back to adolescence.

"I am told," whispered Ughtred solemnly, "that at first blush, this seemed like being a total and unqualified success. The people, with their usual disregard of their own true advantages, had allowed the Intellectuals to insinuate themselves into almost every position of real power. It appeared that the editor of almost every national daily was really — though often secretly — an Intellectual. The BBC was completely under their control. Even the armed forces had, during the last war, let themselves be hoodwinked into believing that wars couldn't be won without the application of brain-power. This unhappy belief, which was found to have permeated almost the whole community, nearly proved its undoing."

"Then what happened?" breathed James, really excited now.

"There ensued," Ughtred said, "ten days that shook the world. The public at first was totally and absolutely confused. They knew that they had long been wanting something exciting to happen — and now something had, which inevitably made them think that what happened must have been what they wanted. But it wasn't."

"Clearly not," James agreed.

"The Intellectuals," Ughtred continued, "apparently went delirious with organization. They cut out the Light Programme of the BBC and substituted continuous editorial comment by Mr. Kingsley Martin. They turned all the strip cartoons into illustrations of intellectual activity. They organized WEA lectures in every village hall and showed foreign films in every cinema. But two things they forgot."

"What were they?" begged James.

"The police," said Ughtred, "and M.I. 5."

James expostulated. "But look here! I met some of those M.I. 5 blokes during the war. If *they* weren't Intellectuals, I don't know *what* they were."

"Ah, during the war," agreed Ughtred. "But as soon as it was over, M.I. 5 was virtually the only organization really to set its house in order, though it seems that this happened by accident. Apparently M.I. 5 embarked on an anti-Communist drive in 1946, and being quite unable to distinguish between Intellectuals and Communists, cleared out both."

James heaved a sigh of relief. "Good for them," he commented quietly. "And then what happened?"

"Naming themselves finally and decisively the Tory Party," continued Ughtred, "the group of politicians I have mentioned went into action. They had M.I. 5, they had the police, and, most important of all, they had the police horses. No Englishman, as you know, will do anything against a police horse. And, fortunately for the Tories, one of the Intellectuals *did*. He struck at the leg of a police horse with his briefcase while being hustled out of the Central Office of Information. The widest publicity was given to the incident and from that moment, of course, Sir W—— S—— and his party had won hands down."

"Naturally," agreed James. "And what became of the Intellectuals?"

"Well, after the Election," concluded Ughtred " — which resulted in an absolutely phenomenal popular mandate for the Tories — they disappeared. Many of them clearly made up their minds to the inevitable and are making out as best they can under the new régime. But it is said," and here Ughtred lowered his voice still further, "that some of them have gone underground."

All this information was too astounding to be assimilated immediately. James poured himself out another glass of sherry, and sat sipping it for a minute or two in silence.

"But look here," he said suddenly, "all this that you've been telling me doesn't explain the absolutely fantastic things that have been happening to me ever since I landed." He thought of the cherry-cheeked maid and blushed.

At this moment the door opened and a bunch of members came in. Neither James nor Ughtred liked to con-

tinue their conversation until the room had filled up
sufficiently for them to speak unheard.

"The trouble is," Ughtred at last went on, "that I
really don't know much more than I've told you. I got
all that information out of old copies of *The Times* last
night and really, I was so sleepy by the time I'd got so
far, that I just gave it up and went to bed. But I must
agree that a great many things remain inexplicable and
I certainly should like to know more about them."

"I've *got* to know," said James irritably, when at that
moment he caught sight of a familiar face entering the
room.

"Mr. Hardiman!" he exclaimed, jumping up, and Mr.
Hardiman, for it was he, said with apparent pleasure,
"Well, well, very pleasant. Didn't think I'd meet you
again so soon."

"Let me introduce you," said James. "My friend,
Mr. Thicknesse, who came back to England with me.
Ughtred, this is Mr. Hardiman whom I met on the train
yesterday."

"I am delighted to make your acquaintance," said
Ughtred with his usual courtesy. "Won't you sit down
and take a glass of sherry with us?"

"Very cordial of you," said Mr. Hardiman, and the
three gentlemen sipped their sherry and talked amicably about cricket, a subject that, James was delighted
to notice, seemed altogether unfraught with topical embarrassment.

At last the decanter was empty and Mr. Hardiman said, "Come and let's lunch together," and after a little polite parleying, Ughtred and James were following their host into the dining-room.

On the way, Ughtred whispered to James, "I am of the opinion that this fortunate meeting may prove to be the very source of information that we were needing."

"Quite," said James with a certain pride, and they moved to a small table for three against the wall.

❉   ❉   ❉

The mulligatawny, the steak-and-mushroom-pie and the Welsh rabbit had all gone down very well. The gentlemen were sipping their coffee when Ughtred, in response to an appealing glance from James, at last diverted the conversation from tiger-hunting in the Hindu Kush.

"Hardiman," he said, "my young friend and I, who have, as you know, returned to England as virtual strangers, were wondering whether you would be so very kind as to explain to us the principles behind the many puzzling incidents that have beset us since we landed."

"Delighted," said Mr. Hardiman cordially. "Anything you want to know."

"Well, I want to know about *this*," broke in James impetuously, fishing his gold disc out of his pocket and flinging it on the table before them.

"Oh, grading," said Mr. Hardiman. "That's perfectly simple." James and Ughtred turned eagerly expectant faces towards him.

"You know, don't you," asked Mr. Hardiman, "that the Government we have now was elected to do away with all that nasty equality bosh?"

"So I've heard," agreed Ughtred cautiously.

"It's perfectly simple," repeated Mr. Hardiman, "only an extension — what you might call a formalization — of the fundamental principles underlying British society as a whole. It's — now what was it the Prime Minister called it? — ah, yes, I have it — it's the perfect flowering of the class system." He looked complacently at his audience as if awaiting applause and Ughtred, seeing that something was expected of them, murmured politely, "Very apt."

But James was more impatient. "What *I* want to know," he said, "is how it works."

"Just as you'd expect," replied Mr. Hardiman. "The whole population has been formally divided into the five classes that it naturally comprises. Each class has, of course, its own distinctive outlook and way of life and, with those, different privileges and compensations. People like to know where they are, you see, and they like to know where other people are, too.'

"I can quite see," commented Ughtred, "that such a classification must save a great deal of exploratory talk when strangers meet in trains. How exactly does this admirable system work?"

"Well, there's A's," began Mr. Hardiman, ticking it off on his little fingers. "We're all A's, of course, or we wouldn't be here. Its hard to say just what makes an A, though you can tell one when you meet him. Birth, of course, and certain positions like the administrative grade of the Civil Service. Then there's money, though that's not enough by itself; you have got to have an attitude of easy superiority as well."

James and Ughtred looked at each other in surprise too deep for words. Gradually, over the face of each, an enormous complacent smile unconsciously spread. Ughtred said slowly: "Do you know, I find this a most exciting and satisfactory concept."

"We all did," said Mr. Hardiman, "we all did."

James had suddenly remembered Martin and his face fell. He said glumly, "I suppose University Dons and these sorts of people are all A's, too."

"By no means," expostulated Mr. Hardiman. "I will admit that such was the original intention, but after the" — he lowered his voice — "after the *trouble,* it was found that the weeding out of pernicious doctrinaires had deprived the Universities of almost half of their senior members. The situation is gradually being rectified, of course, by judicious appointments, and it is intended that eventually Dons will automatically become A's on appointment. But at present it's impossible. I can assure you that the White Paper analysing the origins and opinions of University staffs appalled the whole nation." He shook his head gravely in shocked reminiscence.

"There is a great deal more that I should like to ask about A's," Ughtred said, "but for the moment I think it would be simpler for me and my young friend if you were briefly to indicate something of the other four grades."

"B's," responded Mr. Hardiman, "represent the middle classes. At its lower level you will find the white-collar clerk, at the top the sort of business men who live in expensive houses in outer suburbs."

"I understand perfectly," said Ughtred. He pondered a moment and asked, "What about the Church?"

"RC's and Church of England padres A," said Mr. Hardiman succinctly. "All others B's."

"The Forces?" queried James.

"A bit more complicated. Navy A, Air Force B — I'm speaking only of officers, of course — and Army according to rank and regiment. I should add, however, that all permanent NCO's of ten years' standing automatically become C's — I'll tell you what those are in a minute."

"Interesting," commented Ughtred, "because it's just what I should have expected."

"Of course," Mr. Hardiman said impatiently, "its just what anyone would expect — that's the beauty of it. There's nothing artificial anywhere. Shall I go on?"

Ughtred and James murmured, "Please do."

"Now C's. C's," said Mr. Hardiman with enthusiasm, "are a very interesting class. Where B's have silver discs, C's have solid English oak, and that's thoroughly symbolic. C's are the servants of A's."

Ughtred asked politely: "In what sense?"

"Why in almost every sense. As I said to you yesterday, Mr. Leigh-Smith," he turned to James, "chaps like serving Sahibs. C's are people who've *chosen* to wait on A's just to be in touch with them — waiters, hairdressers, butlers, housekeepers, and agricultural workers on big estates."

"It's quite true," Ughtred murmured, almost to himself. "They *are* a separate class."

"Of course it's true," said Mr. Hardiman almost wearily. "Haven't I told you already that the whole thing's absolutely natural and true?"

"I beg your pardon," Ughtred said. "Please continue. You were about to deal with the D's."

"D's," said Mr. Hardiman, "wear bronze discs and are Trade Unionists."

"Trade Unionists!" broke from Ughtred and James simultaneously, "but — "

Mr. Hardiman held up his hand. "I know what you're going to say," he protested, "but you're wrong. Under proper treatment the Trade Unions have been happy to revert to their natural status which is, of course, that of being the most conservative body in the country."

"But don't you have a lot of strikes?" Ughtred asked.

"Hardly," replied Mr. Hardiman, smiling gently, "since we not only re-enacted the Trade Disputes Act but Pitt's Combination Acts as well, thus making all strikes, with the exception of employers' lock-outs, illegal."

"Masterly," murmured Ughtred, struck with admiration.

"E's," continued Mr. Hardiman, "wear lead discs and comprise, if I may borrow a vulgar but picturesque phrase, the odds and sods. No privileges at all, of course. Tramps, casuals and, of course, any such" — he lowered his voice again — "any such Intellectuals as the police may happen to pick up." James thought of Martin and felt a moment's savage joy, but Mr. Hardiman added. "Of course, most of them knew which side their bread was buttered and settled down more or less happily to being B's." He chuckled. "It's not easy to be an Intellectual among the B's," he said.

All three faces broke into sadistic grins. Mr. Hardiman looked at his watch. "Got to push along now," he said. "Promised a chap to make up a four. Well, it's been most interesting talking to you. Hope to see you again soon." With a cordial smile, he hustled off.

❖   ❖   ❖

Ughtred murmured: "There's a great deal more I should have liked to have asked, but no doubt we shall find it all out in due course."

"I jolly well hope so," said James. "Pretty exciting, don't you think?"

"Indeed, yes," agreed Ughtred, "though natural when you come to think of it. The English have always been sound at heart, you know, and they've never really believed that Jack's as good as his neighbour — not unless, that's to say, they themselves happen to be Jack. Most people's ambition is to better themselves, and you can't do that unless there's someone better than you."

"But there's no one better than us," James said with sudden elation. "Ughtred, do you realize what's happened? There's no one better than us. Not rotten shop stewards nor clever types nor educated women nor jumped-up board-school boys. We're tops!" He looked at Ughtred with triumphant ecstasy and then, in a more normal voice, added, "What shall we do next?"

"I, myself," said Ughtred, "was directed to this admirable club by the Custom's official yesterday — but they told me this morning that some rooms in the Albany are being prepared for me. I understand they once used to belong to Miss G. B. Stern, but naturally no writers, let alone women, are allowed there now. And I have," he added with pride, "an invitation to pay a week-end visit to Lady Wendover who is giving a house party at her lovely house in Buckinghamshire. When I last left England, she had just turned over the house to the nation, what with death duties and so on; but I imagine that things are different now." He sighed happily and asked James: "What are *you* going to do?"

"Well, *I've* got some rooms near here," James said proudly. "So I thought I'd go and inspect them and then go down to Surrey for the week-end and see my parents. They've got a place at Hindhead, you know."

"And I am sure they will be delighted to see you," Ughtred said cordially. "May I suggest that we meet here again on Monday for lunch? By that time, we should both have discovered a great many interesting things and we could pool our separate experiences to the advantage of both." James readily agreed and with mutual good wishes they parted.

*   *   *

It was while sauntering down St. James's Street to his new address that James found his eye caught and held by the motor-car showroom. With three thousand a year, he thought quickly, I *could* — and before he knew where he was he was inside the showroom and a salesman of grave and dignified demeanor had approached him.

"What I'd thought of," James said somewhat nervously, "was something like one of the old Lagondas — you know, the sort with outside tubes and a strap round the bonnet — but I believe everything's streamlined these days." He cursed himself for a fool. After all, outside pipes and what not *were* rather adolescent, but damn it, thought James, I've always wanted a car like that and why not? He waited anxiously for the salesman's reply.

"I believe," the salesman was saying smoothly, "that we have the very model you are looking for. So many gentlemen like yourself have expressed just such a preference, that Lagondas have made a special model to suit them. If you will come this way, sir." He led James through a maze of limousines and coupés — and there, standing by itself, was the car of James's dreams. Not only had it outside pipes and a strap round the bonnet — it had a searchlight and a wireless mast and outside gears and a rev counter and a fantail exhaust and even, as the salesman demonstrated, a melodious Continental horn.

The salesman was saying, "She's a beauty, isn't she? Of course, she's only allowed to be sold to A's; I take it that that part of it would be all right?" He looked questioningly at James who, somewhat confused, fumbled for his disc and displayed it to the salesman.

For a few moments both men stood apparently rapt in ecstasy at the sight of the lovely machine. Then James managed to stutter out, "What does she — I mean what's the price?"

"Three thousand," said the salesman.

James asked, "Does that include Purchase Tax?"

The salesman said almost reproachfully, "No purchase tax for A's." He stole a quick look at James, then added, "Of course we wouldn't press for payment all at once. If you could let us have, say, five hundred on account and the rest eventually, we would find that perfectly satisfactory."

James gulped and said, "I'll take it." Then he asked, "What's the delay before delivery?"

This time the salesman began to look as if he thought James was mad. "No delay at all, sir, for A's," he explained. "If you like, we can get it out right away and you can drive off in it."

"Gosh, I'd like that," James said excitedly. He pictured himself arriving at Beechmeads in this magnificent automobile. Then his face fell — he felt constrained to explain. "But I'm afraid I can't. You see, I've only just arrived in England and I haven't had time yet to go and see my bank manager and fix things up."

The salesman waved this away. "But we shouldn't dream of troubling you for your cheque until it's convenient to you," he protested. "If you will simply let us have your name and address, everything will be perfectly all right."

So James went to a little office and produced the card the Ministry had given him and the salesman copied down his new address. When he emerged, it was to find the Lagonda waiting for him in the street outside.

One last thought struck him, but he was not anxious to make a fool of himself again.

"I take it," he said hesitantly, "that there's no petrol rationing for A's?"

"None at all," the salesman agreed blandly, and James engaged his clutch, put his gear lever into first, and was off.

Chapter 5

JAMES HAD NEVER KNOWN himself so happy as he was that fine spring afternoon whizzing down the Portsmouth road. He had inspected his new rooms, made himself acquainted with Mr. and Mrs. Crabtree, who kept the superior gentelmen's chambers in which they were, and arranged that his luggage should be collected from the Coningsby and his bill paid. Now, without a care in the world, he was whistling "Lily Marlene" (which the island radio had been forever picking up from one set of combatants or the other) and wondering what sort of set-up he would find at Beechmeads.

It was not in James's nature to notice the appearance of the countryside or to comment on the architectural features of village or town as he passed through them. The Portsmouth road seemed very much the same as it had always been and James, entirely lacking in any sociological curiosity, had no mind to wonder what overt changes this new political system might have made.

The Lagonda had been running so smoothly that it was with something approaching regret that James slowed it up as he came to the thick hedges of Beechmeads. "They've painted the gate," he commented, as he got out of the car and pushed it open, a wide white wooden gate that recalled, as it was meant to, the lesser entrance to some great estate. "They've re-

gravelled the drive," he noticed, as he drove slowly
along the hundred yards of wide path dignified by that
name. And finally, "How smart everything looks!" he
exclaimed as he pulled up before the bright red bricks
of Beechmeads' twentieth-century façade, stopped in
front of the white Queen Anne porch, and hooted his
melodious French horn.

Let other pens cope with tender sentiment and true
emotions! Mine must pass over the domestic passions
evoked by James's unexpected return from what his
family had assumed the grave to be a polite synonym,
and present him to you again as he sits with them in
the half-panelled hall.

James's mother, a glass of sherry in her hand ("You'll
be making your old mother drunk," she had exclaimed
playfully), sat as near the prodigal as she could, her
eyes feasting tenderly on his handsome bronzed face.
His elder brother, Rodney — who had been articled to
a solicitor in Guildford and was said, when James left,
to be making out quite well — was stretched out in an
armchair, a pipe between his teeth and two spaniels at
his feet; James noticed his well-cut tweeds with surprise and looked with a certain distaste on his sister
Joyce who was wearing, as she had been when he left,
a pair of shabby riding-breeches and a hand-knitted
jersey of fantastic and squandered intricacy. James's
father, retired from stock-broking these many years,
stood in his habitual position before the fireplace, a re-
production Jacobean glass of whisky in his hands.

James had, of course, to tell his Odyssey many times over, and loud were the exclamations and question as he revealed each stage of it. It must be admitted that in James's account many incidents and characters became transposed so that he himself appeared as the Admirable Crichton throughout. But which of us would do less in the bosom of our homes?

"What a moment it must have been for you," remarked Mrs. Leigh-Smith at last, "when you set foot in old England again."

"I'll say it was," and James said this with feeling. "It was one of the biggest shocks of my young life."

His family glanced at each other oddly, but before any further comments could be made, a loud gong reverberated through the house. "Damn," said all the family, and James asked, "What the devil's that?"

"The dressing-gong," said his father, and his mother added, "You'd better go up and change now, dearest boy. I'm sure you'll find your evening clothes laid out in your old room."

What an odd way of putting it, thought James. Aloud he said, "Don't you think we could skip changing tonight and have some more drinks instead?"

His father said loudly, "Ruddy good idea!" and then looked, James thought, apprehensively at his mother who said, "I really don't think we'd better. We've got to be careful, you know, since the last warning," and James's father looked sheepish and followed his wife upstairs.

❈   ❈   ❈

Outside his bedroom door, James said to Rodney, "What's all this about last warnings? Sounds rather like witches'-curse stuff to me," and Rodney looked embarrassed and said, "Oh, you'll hear about it all soon enough," and hurried away to his room.

❀   ❀   ❀

It was, James admitted as he tied his black tie, rather a pleasure to be in civilized clothes again. He looked into his wardrobe and was pleased to see that some of his old suits still hung there in quite reasonable condition. I'll take them back to town with me, he decided, to wear until I can get something decent, and he contemptuously hurled the Castaways' Charitable offering into a corner and resolved to have no more to do with it.

❀   ❀   ❀

He was still further pleased to find that a fresh tray of drinks was waiting when he came down again to the lounge hall. His sister Joyce was already there, in one of those full-skirted taffeta dresses that, despite their unsuitability for any female over fourteen years, have long been recognized as almost obligatory in England for unmarried girls. Then the rest of the family came down, James's mother looking so nice in her black lace that James impulsively put his arm around her and said, "By Jove, it's good to be home again."

He heard Joyce mutter, "Long may you think so,"

and then a slim dark butler appeared and announced that dinner was served.

*　　*　　*

Dinner, James found, was rather an uncomfortable meal. For one thing the butler (whose name, he discovered, was Reynolds) was perpetually there, silent enough and deft enough, but a strangely obtrusive personality for all that. For another, there were *so* many courses — and all so dull and so badly cooked. James waded through an imperfectly cut grapefruit, some gravy soup, some boiled turbot, a partridge, a saddle of mutton, a gooseberry tart, some soggy mushrooms, and then, uncomfortably replete, ventured, "You do eat rather a lot these days, don't you?"

"Hush," said his mother instantly and hurriedly made still another of those remarks on the weather and its relation to the garden that had formed the staple topic of conversation throughout dinner. Reynolds removed the plates and an immense épergne of fruit was placed on the table. Mrs. Leigh-Smith toyed faintly with a few grapes and at last, with something approaching relief, said, "Come, Joyce," and the ladies left the room.

Now, relieved of the ladies and the butler, a more easy atmosphere settled on the company. James sipped his port and puffed at the excellent cigar his father had offered him. At last he said, "Why *do* you eat so much?"

"It's the servants," his father said wearily. "They're

genuine C's, of course, so they won't be satisfied with less."

"We'll get used to it in time," Rodney said encouragingly, and Mr. Leigh-Smith said, "I suppose so. But if you knew how much I look back to those happy days during the war when we used to open a tin of baked beans in the kitchen."

James, a little out of his depth, ventured, "Of course, if they cooked it better —"

"It's no use," said his father. "It's the traditional English home cooking, my boy, and we've just got to put up with it." He sighed heavily and said, "Shall we join the ladies?"

*   *   *

They found Mrs. Leigh-Smith and Joyce boiling up the Cona in the drawing-room. The evening passed like all those James had remembered in the past. For a time, Mrs. Leigh-Smith stitched at her tapestry and Joyce knitted at yet another of her appalling pullovers. Then Mr. Leigh-Smith said, "What about a little game?" and for the next ten minutes everyone counted deficient packs of cards until at last they found two with fifty-two cards each and played vingty for matches until punctually at ten Reynolds brought in a tray of drinks. Soon Mrs. Leigh-Smith got up and started patting cushions into place and at last went up to bed, followed by her husband and daughter and leaving the two brothers alone. "Now don't you two boys stay yarning until all hours," she had said playfully as she went, which so inhibited them that for the first ten minutes they both sat silently smoking.

At last Rodney refilled his pipe and asked, "What do you think of things?"

"The new régime? I think it's wizard," James said enthusiastically, and then, as Rodney made no response, "Why? Don't you?"

There was another pause. Rodney muttered, "I suppose that fellow's gone to bed. One can never be quite sure." He listened intently for a minute or two, and then said, "We all thought it was going to be, you know. But it's not so easy as it sounds."

"Why not?" asked James.

"Well," said Rodney. "Take me. When it started, they said I'd got to leave the office. Being a solicitor, they said, wasn't suitable for an A, not unless it was one of those superior firms in London and then it had got to be hereditary. At first, of course, I was delighted. No more office, I said, plenty of time to be in the open air, play golf and what not — well, anyone would have been pleased, wouldn't they?"

"I should say so," agreed James.

"But it began to pall," said Rodney sadly. "There's not much to do round here, you know, and I'd never had a chance to make any pals outside the office. So in the end I went up to town and saw the Ministry — you've been there, I suppose, James?" James nodded and Rodney resumed his story.

"They seemed quite reasonable to begin with," he said " 'What would you like to do?' they asked, and I said, straightaway, because I'd been thinking about it quite a bit, that I'd like to be a land agent on some big estate. And I would, you know," he said with a certain pathos. "I'm good at open-air things and I'm interested and the bit of law I've done would have come in quite handy. I do really think I could have made a success of it."

"I'm sure you would," James said warmly. "It sounds like a winner to me. I'd have thought they'd have fixed you up in no time. What went wrong?"

"Primogeniture," said Rodney, and then, as James looked startled, "Oh, yes, primogeniture, that's what they said and they kept on saying it. Eldest sons, they said, had got to think of their dignity. What would happen, they said, if eldest sons just went out and worked like anyone else? Why couldn't I just stay at home, they asked, and run the estate, and wait to inherit? Well, I said that Beechmeads wasn't big enough to need much running and they said in that case why didn't I come up to town and run about a bit? They'd soon fix me up, they said."

"Well, why didn't you?" asked James, thinking with pleasure of all the fixing up that had been done for him.

"I didn't want to," Rodney said irritably. "I can't stick town life — I never could. I made that all perfectly clear to them and in the end they said they'd see what they could do."

James asked eagerly, "And did they?"

"That," said Rodney, "is just the trouble. They did."

James looked expectant.

"You remember the old Grange?" said Rodney and waited.

James remembered the old Grange all right. How many times had he not boasted of it at school, the old family home in Derbyshire, amid its acres of barren moor, that the Leigh-Smith family had, in James's early childhood, been forced to abandon for lack of the necessary resources to make it habitable. "I thought it was taken over by an approved school," he said.

"It was," said Rodney. "But after I'd been to see them, the Ministry went and requisitioned it back again. They've got the powers to do that, you know, where old county families have had to sell their homes to unsuitable people. They're very keen, of course, on re-establishing the old social life of the counties and the long and short of it is that we had an official letter yesterday, suggesting that we should all go and live there again. Of course, they'd provide the wherewithal to do it up and buy hunters and so on. They say so."

"And how do you feel about it?" asked James. It seemed a splendid idea to him. He had always been a little ashamed of the almost suburban smugness of Beechmeads, and could readily picture himself asking new friends up to the family place in Derbyshire for a spot of shooting.

Rodney said slowly, "For myself, you know, I'd like

it very much. In fact, it would suit me down to the ground. But mother and dad have been heart-broken since the letter arrived, and I don't like to press them."

James said in astonishment, "You must have got them wrong. Don't you remember, when we were kids, how they used to grumble about Beechmeads and say how we'd all go back to the Grange as soon as our ship came home?"

Rodney fidgeted and looked at the floor and then said, "The war's made a lot of difference to them. You wait till you have a proper talk to them and you'll see for yourself. Besides, there's Joyce."

"Good old Joyce," said James, and burst out laughing. "Still as plain as ever."

"Still," Rodney remonstrated, "the Ministry were perfectly prepared to find her a husband, or, alternatively, enough income and interests to settle down to being the daughter at home."

"And which did she pick?" asked James, still laughing heartily.

"During the war," Rodney said with disgust, "Joyce went as a land-girl on some horrible chicken farm the other side of Haslemere. It now appears that she fell in love with the manager and intended to marry him."

"And — ?" said James questioningly.

"The man's a B," said Rodney, and clamped down his mouth as if that were all that there was to be said.

But James said, "I don't quite get it. What happens if an A marries a B?"

"If it's a man A marrying a B woman," explained Rodney, "it *can* be done, though it's rather frowned on and the wife may get a bad time with other women when she goes into Society. You see, the old English principle applies — a wife takes the status of her husband. So if Joyce goes and marries a B, we could none of us have anything more to do with her."

"Seems a bit harsh," commented James, "but, at the risk of feeling unbrotherly, the prospect of having nothing more to do with Joyce wouldn't distress me unduly."

"Maybe not," said Rodney solemnly, "but it would worry mother, and besides, it wouldn't do us much good in Derbyshire, you know." He knocked out his pipe and stood up, stretching himself. "Sometimes I wish — " he started, then he broke off and the brothers went up to bed.

*   *   *

James was awakened next morning by the parlour-maid — not, he was rather relieved to see, a pretty one — bringing him a lukewarm cup of tea with a couple of Osborne biscuits melting into sogginess in the saucer. "Good-morning, sir," she said, pulling the curtains vigorously and letting the somewhat anaemic light of a fine May morning fall upon James's reluctant face. "What suit would be wishing to wear, sir," she asked, gathering up James's dinner jacket and hanging it deftly in the wardrobe, and on receiving James's mumbled preference for the old brown tweed, she informed him that Mr. Rodney had already bathed and that his bath was drawn and then prepared to leave, stopping only at the door to announce, "Mr. Reynolds has asked me to say, sir, that he has cleaned the twelve-bore, in case you should be wishing to take a walk later, sir."

Hell and damnation, thought James, what the devil does that fool of a butler imagine I'm going to shoot in the two and a half acres of Beechmeads. Resentfully he rolled out of bed and shuffled off to the bathroom where he was forced to realize that not even the new régime could make the inefficient hot-water system produce two hot baths in succession. Then he returned to the bedroom to find the old brown suit neatly laid out with its appropriate accessories, dressed himself, and then, as the hideous cacophony of the gong reverberated again through the house, went down to breakfast.

His mother was already seated behind what James recognized as the Very Best Silver Coffee Set, usually brought out only when his great-aunt, the Countess of Hellions Bumpstead, came to stay. "Halloa," he said, as he kissed her good-morning, "is this in *my* honour?" and she, with that anxious sidelong glance that he was coming to recognize in his family, replied, "Oh, no, dear. We use it every day now. Reynolds polishes it so beautifully and — well, can I give you some coffee, dear?"

James accepted the coffee, helped himself to porridge

and began a hearty breakfast. The other members of the family soon arrived and they all breakfasted in that gloomy silence hallowed by years of tradition, and broken only by Mrs. Leigh-Smith's little comments on her correspondence and the family's uninterested grunts in reply.

At last the main business of eating was over, and cigarettes were lit. Mrs. Leigh-Smith laid down the last of her letters and asked brightly, "And now, what is everyone doing today?"

Joyce instantly looked sullenly down at her plate; the others merely looked blank. James, anxious to be helpful, said, "Well, what were *you* thinking of doing, mamma?"

Mrs. Leigh-Smith immediately looked frightened. She said nervously, "Well, I *ought* to be doing some charity — I know cook has made a batch of calves' foot jelly — but what I was really hoping, James, was that you might find time to walk round the garden with me. I should so much like to show you what the border's been doing."

"I should love to," James said politely, although horticulture bored him to tears. I'll be back in town on Monday, he reflected. I might as well do them proud while I'm here. He turned to his father, "What are you doing, dad?" he asked.

"I shall go to the library," said his father rather loudly, "and get on with my book on seventeenth-century Surrey pediments." In a more normal voice he added, "How'd you like to come along to the pub with me at twelve and get a drink?"

"Love to," said James instantly. At least this would set a *terminus ad quem* to the garden perambulation. But James's mother only looked more frightened than ever and said, "Oh, Frank, you *will* be careful, won't you?"

"We'll be going to the Goat and Compasses," said Mr. Leigh-Smith, again in that unnaturally loud voice that sounded as if he wanted someone to overhear him. "Like to come, too, Rodney?"

"No, thanks," Rodney said, getting up. "I rather thought of going for a long tramp. Try to think things out, you know." He went out of the room and his mother said, "Poor boy, he has a lot on his mind," and then, to James, "I'll meet you in half an hour, then," and for the next half-hour the family separated.

*   *   *

James reached the hall again before his mother and just in time to see his sister Joyce in a shabby raincoat disappearing furtively down a passage. He wondered whether to hail her, but decided it was better to let her go her way. I suppose she's off to her chicken farmer, he thought, pity there's got to be all this secrecy about it, and then turned to find his mother standing by him, thick shoes on her feet and a shapeless straw hat pinned on to the top of her head.

"I'm ready now, dear," she said brightly. "Shall we start off down the drive?"

*　　*　　*

The conversation that ensued during the next hour and a half will be so well known to all gardeners that it is unnecessary to rehearse it. Let it suffice to say that by the end of that time James and his mother had "done" the drive, the shrub border, the mixed border, the vegetable garden and the rock garden, had looked at the new clematis, wondered whether the ceanothus had survived the winter, decided that if there weren't any late frosts they'd have more apples than they'd know what to do with, and were now seated on the rustic seat at the end of the tennis lawn.

"I see that the cypress hedge has shot up quite a bit since I was last home," said James, pointing to a dark straggly growth that divided Beechmeads from its neighbour. "It doesn't look as if the Appelbaums can see through now."

"No," agreed his mother, "at least, that's to say, they couldn't anyway. We've got some new people next door now. The Applebaums have gone."

"Oh, really," said James with interest, "I thought they were here for keeps. What became of them?"

"You see, this is an A area," Mrs. Leigh-Smith explained, "and being Jews, of course they had to go. I believe they're living in Golders Green now."

"Whew!" exclaimed James, "you do surprise me. Are all Jews B's then?"

"All except the Rothschilds and a couple of other families," said Mrs. Leigh-Smith, "and they were made A's in compliment to Disraeli."

"That all seems pretty sound," remarked James who, in common with most young men of his age and class, was mildly anti-Semitic. "Anyway, you must be pretty relieved to have got rid of the Appelbaums, what? Remember how furious we used to get when they played that ghastly gramophone of theirs till all hours?"

But his mother didn't respond as he'd expected. "I don't know," she said. "You mustn't tell anyone I said so, but father and I do rather miss them. You see, Rachel Appelbaum and I worked together at the Red Cross during the war, and what with father and Sidney both liking to talk about business at the Home Guard, well, we all got very friendly. We used to play bridge together once a week and father and I both used to look forward to our Wednesday evenings. In fact, we miss the Appelbaums quite a lot."

James was completely astounded. When he had last been at home, his parents had constantly been inveighing against the Appelbaums, telling everyone who would listen how it brought the neighbourhood down to have Jews living in it and that it oughtn't to be allowed. And now it wasn't allowed — and apparently both his parents were sorry. James couldn't make head or tail of it.

"I imagine you haven't got much time to miss them," he said consolingly. "What's all this charity you were talking about?"

But his mother did not look, as he had intended, consoled. Instead she said despairingly, "That's another of my worries. The Government want all ladies in my position to do a lot of charity, visit the poor with blankets and calves' foot jelly and send them coals in the winter; in fact, they issue us with special coals for the purpose. Well, of course, you're only supposed to do charity to C's, and there aren't nearly as many C's around here as there are A's. We're all supposed to go at least once a month and the consequence is, all the C's are getting more blankets than they could possibly use. And as for the calves' foot jelly — they just won't touch it since they've tasted Heinz's tomato soup." She sighed deeply and James, at a loss for words, sighed with her.

"What would happen if you just didn't do it?" he asked anxiously.

"Oh, we'd get into trouble," said Mrs. Leigh-Smith hurriedly. "We've been warned once — though I can't tell you about that, you must ask father — and though there are disadvantages to everything, of course, if we're born A's, then it's our duty to live up to it, isn't it?"

"I suppose so," said James. He was feeling a little uncertain. As far as he could make out, his mother now had everything she had continually grumbled about before the war — money, servants, position, dignity, a chance to do good. Why did she seem so unhappy about it?

As if in answer to his thoughts, she now said, "Sometimes I almost wish that all this had never — " She broke off in alarm as footsteps came crunching along the gravel behind them. "If that's Reynolds — " she began in a low agitated whisper and then, in a very loud unnatural voice, "So you see, darling, just how happy we all are under the new régime." She sat for a minute, taut and expectant, then suddenly relaxed as she heard her husband's voice booming behind her.

"Halloa, you two," it broke in genially. "Look here, Muriel, if you've finished showing this boy of ours all your pet rock-plants, I'm going to take him off to the local and fill him up with beer."

"I'm quite ready if mother can spare me now," said James, rising in some relief. What could be the matter with his mother? Her nerves seemed to be in a shocking state, and sometimes her words and behaviour were quite unaccountable.

*   *   *

"It's a funny thing," said his father suddenly, as they turned out of the gate, "but since the new régime came in, I've been beginning to get distinct twinges of gout."

James said with that insincere sympathy of the egotist, "Have you been to see anyone about it?"

"Your mother pushed me off to some big man in

London," said Mr. Leigh-Smith, slashing at some dandelions with his stick, "but he didn't do me any good, for all the five guineas he rooked me for it."

"What did he say?" asked James, without much interest.

"Apparently he'd had any number of such cases among A's since the new régime came in," replied his father in a slightly hurt tone. "He didn't show much interest. He just said that it was an occupational disease and I'd got to put up with it." In gloomy silence, he trampled along the road into Hindhead, while James fell into a pleasant reverie in which St. James's and Lagondas and dinner hostesses were all mixed up together.

As they came into the outskirts of Hindhead, Mr. Leigh-Smith suddenly looked up and gave a delighted shout. "Why, if it isn't old Bouncer!" he shouted, waving madly at a little man in grey flannel trousers on the other side of the street, and the little man looked up and called in delighted accents ,"Hallo, you old — " and then stopped dead.

To James's surprise, both men broke off their gesticulations of pleasure with awkward abruptness. Mr. Leigh-Smith whispered, "Come on, James, quickly," and shuffled hastily off down the street, while on the other pavement the little man also hurriedly pursued his way, his eyes fixed on the ground.

James, looking around in surprise, could see no reason why this promising interchange of greetings should thus have been broken off short. All seemed normal, from the sauntering groups of pedestrians to the policeman who was now approaching them, gazing at the little scene with a somewhat sardonic stare. James turned to his father and began, "Whatever — ?" but his father stopped him, muttering urgently, "For God's sake talk about something else." This inevitably reduced James to silence, and as the policeman passed them, they were talking of nothing at all.

His father said out of the corner of his mouth, "I'll explain to you later. Just try to look natural." James looked back and caught the eye of the policeman who just at that moment seemed to be looking back, too. Confused, he turned hurriedly and marched along by the side of his father.

Soon they came to one of those red-brick edifices readily recognizable to the practised eye as a brewery company's incursion into the field of applied design. James remarked, "What do you say we turn in here?" thinking with nostalgia of the light oak tables and the red leather-seated chairs, the embossed galleons on the walls and the marble lino on the floor.

But his father said in a shocked voice, "We can't go in there — it's for B's." James, beginning to get a little irritated, started to say, "Well, we used to — " but Mr. Leigh-Smith broke in with, "We can't now, that's all. Besides I promised your mother. Come along," and strode rapidly down the road.

When, however, they reached their destination in a

small side street, James was pleased that his first thirsty impulse had been frustrated, for the Goat and Compasses was everyone's dream of an old English hostelry. A gaily painted sign hung over a sturdy oak door and all the façade was a maze of twisted beams and curly bottle-glass.

"Decent-looking hole," said James appreciatively, and then suddenly clutched his father's arm and hissed, "Do you see what I see?"

What James saw was a labourer approaching the pub from the other end of the little street. And what was so strange about this labourer was that instead of the neat blue serge that James had remembered as agricultural week-end wear, he was wearing an elaborately embroidered smock. As this figure came up to James and his father, he pulled at a long forelock of hair that seemed to have been growing over his forehead for the purpose, said in a wheezy voice, "Good-day to 'ee, Squire. Good-day, young sir," and disappeared into the Jug and Bottle.

James burst into a wild gust of laughter. Between its paroxysms, he gasped, "I haven't seen anything so funny since the last May Day pageant," and then fell to slapping his thighs and laughing again.

Mr. Leigh-Smith said harshly, "I don't see anything so funny. The smock has been revived as the recognized dress for agricultural labourers."

James managed to say weakly, "However do they get the poor devils to wear the things?"

"It was done through the Women's Institutes on a bonus system," said Mr. Leigh-Smith curtly. "Now if you've quite finished making a fool of yourself in the public street, shall we go in?"

＊　　　＊　　　＊

James and his father did not, of course, follow the besmocked labourer into the Jug and Bottle, but went into the Saloon Bar next door, an enchanting little room with a red-tiled floor, dark oak settles against the beamed walls, and Toby jugs twinkling in a row above the bar. Two gentlemen in tweed caps were conversing quietly in one corner; otherwise the room was empty save for the innkeeper who stood beaming behind the bar, a long white apron round his ample middle and a fluffy fringe of white hair framing his shiny cranium.

"Good-morning, gentlemen," he said genially as father and son came in. "Very seasonable weather we're having, gentlemen, if I may say so. Now what can I get you?"

James and his father each chose a mild-and-bitter, which was slapped on to the counter in polished pewter tankards. Then, Mr. Leigh-Smith having paid with a gold half-sovereign, they took up their drinks and retired to a secluded corner.

"I wish you'd tell me," James ventured, seeking for non-controversial ground, "just how this money system works. Aren't there any pound and ten shilling notes any more?"

"Oh, yes, indeed there are," said Mr. Leigh-Smith, seizing with apparent relief at this topic. "Gold money is only issued to A's; no one else is allowed to use it."

"Then why does everyone accept it, if it's no use to them?" asked James.

"They're bound to accept it," Mr. Leigh-Smith said. "They can change it at any bank for paper money for their own uses. As a matter of fact, all this gold was a present from America to the new régime. Officially, of course, it's only on loan."

"Loan or not, it's much pleasanter to handle than notes," commented James.

"Yes, that's how we all feel," his father said. "Come on, my boy, drink up and let's have another. It's damn good beer they have here."

Over the second pint, James ventured, "I don't quite understand about the status of these pubs. You wouldn't go into the first one because it was a B, and yet that fellow in the smock came in here, too, and you can't tell me *he's* an A."

"Of course not," said his father. This question didn't seem to worry him. "A's and C's go to the same pubs. Why, it would destroy the whole atmosphere of pub life if you couldn't reckon on finding a few C's on the other side of the barrier."

"That's true enough," reflected James. He thought for a moment and asked, "But what about the B's? Wouldn't they like that, too?"

"Oh, no," said Mr. Leigh-Smith decisively. "Rubbing shoulders with other classes isn't a B hobby. Besides, you know, the B's may look like one big group to us, but inside themselves they've got literally thousands of different classes. That's why they like the new régime so much; it seems absolutely natural to them."

"And they don't mind not being A's?" James asked.

"Not a bit," said Mr. Leigh-Smith. "They're always much too busy keeping up their own little barriers inside themselves. Besides, they like the feeling that the gentry are firmly in the saddle. What they didn't like in the old egalitarian days, was not knowing exactly where they and everyone else stood on the social ladder.' He paused for breath. "Come on, my boy, put that one down and we'll have one for the road."

It was not until the third pint was well on its way down that James dared to ask. "Dad, who *was* that bloke we passed on the way down?"

Mr. Leigh-Smith sighed deeply and set his tankard down on the table. "Ah, my boy," he said heavily. "Your mother and I had hoped to keep certain things from you, but I see it's no use. You will have to have the truth."

"Yes, please," said James, a little alarmed by this preamble.

"As you know," Mr. Leigh-Smith began. "Your mother and I have always been staunch Tories. We were frankly appalled by the way things were going between the wars, and we always felt that there'd never be any hope for old England unless something like the new régime came into power."

"I often remember your saying that," agreed James nodding his head, "and when I thought of coming down here yesterday, I was imagining how delighted you'd both be at the way things have turned out. And yet none of you seem a bit happy. What went wrong?"

Mr. Leigh-Smith seemed to be cogitating. "I suppose it was partly the war," he said at last. "We found ourselves mixing with all sorts of peculiar people then, and the funny thing was, we rather liked it. That chap we passed in the street, for instance — he was my Platoon Commander in the Home Guard, and a rare old time we used to have together. Even after the war was over, we all used to meet at that pub down the road for a pint and a good chin-wag. And then — " He stopped.

"And then — " prompted James.

"The new régime came in," said Mr. Leigh-Smith heavily. "My old pals were nearly all of them B's — that chap you saw, for instance, he's manager of the local Woolworth. And, of course, we weren't allowed to mix any more — "

"Not allowed?" broke in James. "How do you mean — not allowed?"

"We've got to stick to our class," said his father miserably. "That's the law. If we don't, we're liable to get degraded. I used to sneak out once or twice and meet the chaps, and then one evening the policeman came up. They're all C's, of course, the police," he added in parentheses. "He was very polite, naturally, but he gave me a pretty sharp hint that I'd have to stick to my own class in future or get into very serious trouble. And it was just after that, that the local Registry Office sent us Reynolds."

"Just who," asked James, "do you think Reynolds is?"

His father glanced hastily round the room and then, leaning forward, put his mouth close to James's ear. "We think," he whispered, "that Reynolds is an M.I. 5 nark."

"Good God!" exclaimed James, really shocked. "I hadn't realized that the new régime depended on that sort of thing."

"They say it's only for a short while," said his father hurriedly. "Just until everyone gets used to it and accepts it as a matter of course. Eventually, they say, all that sort of thing will just wither away."

"I certainly hope so," exclaimed James. "That sort of thing's not very nice, is it?"

Mr. Leigh-Smith was unable to discuss things impersonally for long. "I must admit that your mother and I have been rather worried lately," he said. "We like the district and all that, but we're coming to think we'd do best to accept the Ministry's offer and go off to Derbyshire. As a matter of fact, there are a lot of rumours that they're going to make the whole of Surrey a B area anyway."

"I suppose it really is already," said James reflectively.

"Virtually," agreed his father, "and so we'd have to get out anyway unless we want to be degraded. And — well, I mean to say — one grumbles a bit and so on, but one doesn't really want that, does one?" He ended with a slightly questioning note in his voice.

James said vehemently, "Certainly one doesn't."

"No, I suppose not," said Mr. Leigh-Smith. Was it James's imagination or did he sound disappointed? The conversation soon languished, and after drinking a final pint with the landlord — a courtesy that was, Mr. Leigh-Smith told his son, virtually obligatory — they departed for home.

Chapter 6

IT WAS AFTER CHURCH next morning that James invented an urgent engagement demanding his presence in town that evening. In the past, his family had never been great churchgoers; a couple of visits at Christmas and Easter had about represented their average attendance. Now, James discovered with horror, he had to put on a morning coat and top hat and accompany the rest of his family to church, the servants, headed by Reynolds in black gloves, trotting disciplined in the rear. And then, when they got to the church, James found a huge family pew waiting for them into which he had to file and remain encased for an hour and a half. And so, "I'm rather afraid I'll have to get back to town after lunch," he said, as he sat at table, crumbling his bread.

His family politely urged him to remain, but James could see that they didn't mind that much; they were too taken up with their own troubles. His luggage was packed for him and they all came to the front door to see him off, Joyce still arguing, as she had all day, that she didn't *want* to take her Sunday-school class and she was damned if she was going to. But James could see that all her arguments had the dispirited quality of defeat and that Joyce would undoubtedly take her class this afternoon as she apparently had done every Sunday since the new régime came in.

James felt a weight shift off his shoulders as he turned out of the drive and roared up the hill. Down there, it had been so odd and uneasy that he had been almost beginning to wonder whether things really *were* as rosy as they had first appeared. Now, in his Lagonda on the Portsmouth road, he had no doubts. He started to sing, and with every mile as he neared London, his spirits lifted.

   ❋   ❋   ❋

About six that evening James was sitting in his room, wondering what to do next. He had already admired the decorations and, in particular, the row of German beer-mug stands pinned above the mantelshelf, which were just to his taste. He had approved the books in the little glass-fronted wall bookcase — *Who's Who, Debrett, A Guide to the Turf,* and some rail and aeroplane timetables. He had answered the little pile of invitations to dinners and dances that he had found waiting for him, and stuck the cards prominently on the mantelpiece. Now, as he was idly turning the pages of *Country Life,* there came a knock at the door.

"Come in," shouted James, and in came a tall fair slim young man, his every line the epitome of aristocracy, from his lean aquiline nose to his slim elegantly shod feet.

"Leigh-Smith?" said the young man, coming forward with a pleasant smile. "I'm Rupert Crooke-Haughton — I've got the rooms above yours. I thought I'd just drop in and make your acquaintance."

"Very neighbourly of you," said James, waving his guest to a chair. "You'll have a sherry, won't you?" He had remembered seeing a decanter of sherry and some glasses in one of the cupboards and now he brought these out.

"Extremely good sherry you keep," said Rupert Crooke-Haughton politely, holding up his glass to the light. "Who's your wine-merchant?"

"I'm afraid I don't know," confessed James. "You see, I only arrived back in England a couple of days ago, and I haven't really had time to get the hang of things properly yet."

"Oh, good show," said his guest with enthusiasm. "Then you're just the man for me. There's nothing I like more than showing newcomers round. Chap who had the rooms before you — he and I used to knock around quite a good bit until he got the Ministry to fix him up with a decent marriage. But I'm steering clear of anything like that for a bit. Too many amusing things to do, what?"

"I'll say," agreed James, and the two young men sat and drank sherry together and discovered a host of mutual acquaintances until Rupert Crooke-Haughton suddenly said, "I'm getting a bit peckish, aren't you? What do you say to us going out and looking for a bite?"

James said, "That's a very good idea," and the two young men picked up their hats and their umbrellas and went into the street.

✳   ✳   ✳

James had intended to leave the choice of a restaurant to his new friend. But Rupert strolled down Jermyn Street talking of this and that and blandly ignoring restaurants to the right and left of him, and at last James, feeling uncommonly hungry, pointed to a swing-door through which prospective diners were pressing and asked, "What about that one? It looks all right."

"My dear fellow," said Rupert in a horrified voice, "we can't possibly go there. That's an AB."

"ABC, do you mean?" said James, conscious of having made some appalling gaffe.

"No, an AB," retorted Rupert, "Oh, I forgot — you've only just come home, haven't you?"

"I'm afraid so," said James humbly as they walked on. "What *is* an AB restaurant?"

"Well, it's really a ramp," said Rupert with a superior smile. "You know what B's are. Once in a way, they like to have a bust, go to the theatre and dine after, or take their daughters dancing or something like that. Or sometimes the daughters and their young men like to go a bust themselves. Well, when they do that — I suppose it's about once a year — all their snobbish instincts come to the fore and they like to go somewhere swell. That's why the AB restaurants were invented."

"Oh, I see," said James, "somewhere where A's and B's can both go."

"Not exactly," said Rupert, "though that's what the B's think they are. In fact, no A would dream of going to an AB restaurant, but when the B's get there, all dressed in their best, they take it for granted that everyone else they see there is an A, and they all feel quite happy."

"It's quite a cunning scheme," said James with admiration.

"Quite natural," said Rupert, "just a modification of what naturally tended to happen, like most of the new régime." While they were talking, he had been leading James through a maze of side streets until finally they came to a modest façade behind which was situated, he assured James, one of the best restaurants in London.

＊　　　＊　　　＊

Certainly James found nothing to complain of in the sumptuous meal that was set before him nor in the service that accompanied it. Meanwhile, the two young men had become fast friends, so much so, indeed, that by the time the coffee was put on the table, he had dared to ask Rupert just how a man-about-town was expected to spend his days.

"I'd always thought," he confessed, "that having nothing to do all day would be the most wonderful thing in the world. But not being used to it, I don't know how to set about it, particularly if everyone else is working."

"But everyone else isn't working," protested Rupert. "You must get that idea right out of your head. None of the women are working now, of course, and hardly any of the younger men, unless you'd call being a Guards officer or a rising politician work. We've all got private incomes — why should we?"

"Incidentally," said James as another thought struck him, "just how does the country manage to maintain all us A's? I thought that, after the war, we were all going to be so poor that we'd hardly have enough necessities, let alone the luxuries you and I are enjoying," and he sniffed the bouquet of his Armagnac.

"Ah," said Rupert Crooke-Haughton, "in an egalitarian State that would be true, but as soon as you restore inequalities all sorts of things become possible. Just how many A's do you think there are?"

James shook his head. "I've no idea," he said.

"A tiny number," said Rupert enthusiastically, "a tiny number. You remember how people used to point out that if you took Lord Rothschild's money and divided it among everyone, they'd only get about a farthing each? Well, we found that quite a different situation arose when we took the money from the workers and divided it among *us*. The State can easily afford to give us everything we want, when you consider how much the living-standards of the working classes have been depressed. Before the war, you see, unemployment was pushed down to the bottom of the social scale and the rest of the community were working to maintain the unemployed. Now, the community is still doing that, but the unemployment has been pushed to the top. So you see, you needn't worry about what to do all day, because most of us are as idle as you."

"I'm very glad to hear it," said James greatly relieved. "But do tell me just what sort of things one does?"

Rupert began: "Well, to start with, one usually has one's hatter or one's tailor to see." He glanced delicately at James's old suit, and James blushed and muttered, "Of course." Rupert went on — "and then, if it's fine, one usually walks in the Park and sees people, and sometimes one hires a nag and does a spot of riding oneself. Then there's often a lunch party or else one lunches at one's club or sometimes I have someone to lunch at my rooms. I've got rather a decent collection of etchings," he added with a modest smile, "and lots of girls like to come and see them. Old Mrs. Crabtree's a very decent cook, but, of course, you can only bring A's to your rooms. Everything in its place."

"Of course," echoed James again.

"And then in the afternoon," continued Rupert, "one can go to Hurlingham or to the Academy and one's usually got a certain number of calls to pay. And then there's usually a sherry party and then dinner and a dance or something of that sort — that reminds me," he broke off, "I see you've got a card for the Duchess of Minton's dance tomorrow. Where are you dining first?"

"I believe," said James, trying to remember, "that a Lady de Maltravers has invited me to dine."

"Oh, you're lucky," sighed Rupert. "Sally de Maltravers's dinners are always excellent. I've been roped in by Mary Stanton and I know she'll put me next to that plain daughter of hers. I have a sneaking suspicion that the Ministry have suggested me for a *parti* there, but I'm not playing, no, not even with a record dowry."

"Then we'll meet at the dance," said James who, much as he wanted to enter the gay social whirl, suffered somewhat from shyness — and from the added complication of believing that no one else did.

"Indeed, yes," said Rupert, and called for another glass of brandy.

"Tell me, Rupert," said James curiously, "what did you do before the war?"

An enormous blush mantled Rupert's fair brow. He seemed to be struggling between discretion and honesty, and at last he said, "Promise you won't tell a soul."

"Promise," said James earnestly.

"It's not as if — " stammered Rupert, "I mean, before the war, we were all of us doing some damn funny things, weren't we?"

"I'll say we were," said James with feeling, remembering the Brazilian coffee, the Argentine sheep, the Chilean nitrates, and the rubber in Malaya.

"The Government advises us not to talk about those years," said Rupert. "I'm just telling you in confidence. I was learning how to become a shop-walker at Selfridges."

"Good God!" exclaimed James, really shocked.

"I was really very lucky to get in," said Rupert, who

now seemed to want to disregard the governmental injunction and bare his heart, "mostly they were taking people of social standing *and* first-class degrees, and I only got a third. But someone put in a good word for me and so I got the chance and really," he said with pride, "I was doing quite nicely."

"What was it like?" asked James with interest.

"Rather fun," Rupert said incautiously, and then blushed again and corrected himself, saying: "I mean, of course, that it was absolutely bloody. I say, you know, I think we'd better not talk about these things because sometimes I get rather muddled."

"Righto," agreed James and asked for the bill. "I think we'd better be getting back, anyway."

"But we don't want to go straight back, do we?" protested Rupert.

James said, "Well, if you can think of anything better to do — "

"Easily," said Rupert.

"Only for A's?" queried James.

"Exactly," said Rupert.

And off they went.

Chapter 7

THE NEXT MORNING James awoke early, determined to see to all his affairs and thoroughly settle himself into his new life. He had arranged with Rupert that he would, if he got through his business in time, meet him at the Achilles statue at noon, and so, after a hearty breakfast off two plump and succulent kippers, he made his way into the May sunshine, the Ministry's letters of introduction in his pocket.

Providently, he made his first call that upon his new bank manager, feeling that on the outcome of this visit all the rest would depend. But after half an hour in the manager's private office, he emerged completely reassured, a fat cheque book in one pocket and a fresh supply of sovereigns in another.

In quick succession, then, James visited his barber, his gunsmith, his wine merchant, his hatter, shirtmaker, shoemaker and tailor. These four last, who were clearly accustomed to outfitting gentlemen returned from abroad, were all able to supply him with a sufficiency of other gentlemen's misfits to array him until his own bespoke clothes were ready and it was, consequently, a James wholly debonair who strolled up to the Achilles statue on the stroke of twelve.

Rupert was already waiting for him, a flower in his buttonhole, his neatly gloved hands resting lightly on his silver-topped Malacca stick. He complimented

James on his admirably changed appearance, and together the two young men proceeded to stroll towards Knightsbridge.

Gay indeed was the scene that spread itself before their eyes. The row was filled with thoroughbred horses, their riders all in immaculate black; not a tweed coat, not a bare head was anywhere to be seen. Round and round on the road slowly bowled elegant limousines with here and there an open carriage enclosing lovely ladies in pastel silks with lace-edged parasols shading their complexions from the sun. And up and down the paths surged a merry concourse of the smartest people imaginable — dowagers with their companions and their Pekinese, little boys and girls with coroneted prams and stiffly starched nurses, and, above all, group after group of pretty young ladies and immaculately tailored young men.

Rupert seemed to know everyone there. He was forever stopping to bandy a gay quip with this one or that, and he never failed to introduce James to his friends and acquaintances. James was delighted with the conversation that ensued at each of these *rencontres*. Never in any way the least bit difficult or over his head, it consisted in a species of light badinage with — if the interlocutor were a lady — a flirtatious undertone, and the sallies of laughter that greeted his every quip soon convinced him that he was naturally a brilliant conversationalist. How much pleasanter it is, he reflected, this easy witty interchange, than those awful discussions of Martin's that seemed to be based on nothing but ideas.

At last Rupert proposed that they should sit and rest themselves for a while, and, looking round, perceived a seat occupied only by two young ladies in frilly frocks, their faces hidden by lacy hats. "Why, it's Daisy and Evelyn Marsham!" he explained, and taking James by the arm, he led him over to the two girls and requested their permission to sit down. This being granted, he seated himself by the one called Daisy which left James no choice but to devote himself to the other sister, Evelyn.

How much he regretted this when he was able to steal a glance at Daisy and saw, beneath the brim of her shady hat, the merriest little face imaginable — rose-petal cheeks, tip-tilted nose, wide blue eyes and a mass of golden curls — and heard the now familiar quips being bandied between her and Rupert. How much he regretted it when he looked, in turn, at the dark Evelyn beside him and marked the lowering pout of her discontented lips, the lack-lustre glaze of her eyes. Nor did she in any way respond to the conversational efforts he made, only vouchsafing a sullen "Yes" or "No" to the best that he could offer.

"What a dreadful girl the elder sister is," he said to Rupert after they had made their adieux and were strolling back towards the Dorchester for a quick drink. "How unlike the pretty little Daisy."

"A misfit, I'm afraid," said Rupert sadly, shaking his head. "I'm afraid she'd gone too far for the new régime to be able to have any beneficial effect on her."

"Gone too far!" repeated James, "In what way?" I must admit that he was hoping for some scandalous revelation.

But Rupert disappointed him. "She was in her second year at Oxford when the new régime came in," he explained, "and hoping to become a feature-writer on *Vogue*. Then, of course, as an A, she had to give up both these ideas. The womens' colleges at Oxford automatically became reserved for B's, and journalism, of course, was out of the question."

"Are all journalists B's, then?" asked James.

"Oh, virtually all," responded Rupert. "I believe that Mr. Wentworth Day and one or two others are A's, but there are very few of them. But it didn't really matter *what* Evelyn wanted to be; the point was that, as a female A, she couldn't be anything at all."

"Oh!" said James. Having grown up in a period when nearly all upper-class ladies worked, he found this new concept rather startling.

"The duties of ladies," said Rupert sententiously, in the manner of one repeating a lesson, "are to be gentle and decorative and to marry, after which they must oversee the upbringing of their children, the running of their households, and the welfare of their husbands, promoting this last by every means consonant with feminine modesty and charm."

"Is that a quote?" asked James.

"It is," said Rupert.

"But supposing," suggested James, "that they don't marry?"

"James, you *are* being difficult," said Rupert impatiently. "In an organized society like ours, nearly all of them *do* marry — the Ministry sees to that. And if they don't, there's all kinds of charity work that they're allowed to do, such as arranging dances and fêtes and knitting for seamen and selling flags and — and — " he paused for breath.

" — distributing calves' foot jelly," put in James.

"Exactly," agreed Rupert. "So you see, James, there's no need at all for Evelyn Marsham to go around with that discontented look on her face. But it's my belief," he lowered his voice, "that if it wasn't for her family, she'd apply for degrading and though I know it's naughty to say so, I can't help feeling it might be the best thing all round. After all, one doesn't *like* to see discontented faces, does one?"

James, remembering his experiences at Hindhead, readily agreed that one didn't and the two friends now entered the Dorchester and drank cocktails together until it was time for them to part for their respective lunch dates.

❀   ❀   ❀

Despite the excitement of his many new experiences and acquaintances, James was just as pleased as ever to see Ughtred when he met him at the club for lunch.

He had always respected and admired the older man, even during all those long years on the island, but now, under the new régime, Ughtred radiated such confidence and happiness that it was impossible to meet him without feeling that all must be well with a world that set such a nice man in what was so clearly his right *milieu*. And James, though he would not have admitted it to himself, was beginning to feel the need of a certain reassurance. His visit to his family had shaken him and its effects had not all been dissipated.

But over lunch, James felt his confidence returning. James told Ughtred of his new friend, Rupert Crooke-Haughton, and Ughtred, after he had emerged from a reminiscent search for Rupert's collaterals back to the tenth generation, retaliated with an account of his country week-end which had clearly represented for him the epitome of social bliss.

"By the by," said Ughtred casually, as they sauntered out of the dining-room, "are you free this afternoon?"

"Yes, I am," said James. "Rupert has gone off to pay some calls, but I gather one doesn't have to do that until after one's been entertained, and I don't start being entertained until this evening."

"Then in that case," Ughtred pursued, "I wonder whether you would care to join me in a little excursion I have in mind."

"I should love to," James replied readily. Despite Rupert's ready assurances that a man-about-town had plenty of occupations, James had begun to fear that the coming afternoon might lie heavily on his hands.

"The suggestion I was about to make," Ughtred was saying, "is that we should drop in at one of these Degrading Courts and see just how they work."

James, though less interested than Ughtred in the machinery of government, was quite ready to agree. He had recently heard so many references to the process of degradation that he found himself quite anxious to see what this might entail. Ughtred discovered from the porter that the nearest court likely to be in session was that at Great Marlborough Street, and here they made their way.

❈   ❈   ❈

"I have been finding out a little about these courts," remarked Ughtred as they walked along. "They are presided over by specially appointed magistrates who have, apparently, quite a wide range of powers, though it appears that certain things are beyond their jurisdiction."

"I suppose that magistrates are quite — er — *straight*," ventured James. He didn't quite know why he said this, except that from certain things he had observed about the new régime, it seemed to him that the magistrates might quite well not be.

But Ughtred was horrified. "My dear James," he protested, "you are speaking of British justice. In any case," he added, "there's never any need for a judicature to be what I suppose you would call crooked. The justices are merely there to administer the law; the important thing is the making of the laws that they have to administer, and this aspect of the matter we may reasonably suppose the new régime has well in hand."

"Sorry," muttered James, feeling as he used to when he had been ticked off by his schoolmaster, but Ughtred could never remain outraged for long, and patting James's arm, he observed kindly, "I see we are arrived at our destination. Shall we go in?"

❉   ❉   ❉

Led by a courteous policeman they soon found themselves seated in the front row of the Great Marlborough Street Degrading Court. To James, who had never been in such a place before, the whole scene seemed extremely drab, from the olive-green distemper on the walls to the grey little man who sat high up in the centre of the Court and presided over it. As they took their seats, a plump middle-aged lady, neatly dressed and decorous, was standing in the witness box, apparently being questioned by the magistrate.

"I wonder what this case is about," Ughtred whispered to James, and a near-by policeman who heard him leant over and hissed behind his hand: "Application for re-grading to A — they're just examining the witnesses."

"You are Madame Ada Dixon, proprietress of a

Grade B dress shop in Baker Street?" questioned the magistrate.

"I am," said the witness.

"I believe," said the magistrate, "that the applicant's wife is a regular customer of yours and that you have volunteered to give evidence on her behalf?"

"That's right," said the witness.

"Will you tell your story as simply as possible," the magistrate said.

Madame Dixon began. "Mrs. Waddington has been coming regularly to my establishment for the past twenty years. She's always been a very easy lady to dress, regular B style."

"What," interrupted the magistrate, "is regular B style?"

The witness hesitated. "Well, it's a bit difficult to explain, if you know what I mean," she said doubtfully, "things like embossed velvet — Mrs. Waddington liked a lot of that — and ample cross-overs and modesty vests and plenty of trimmings."

"I see," said the magistrate mendaciously. "Pray proceed."

"But lately," continued the witness, "Mrs. Waddington has completely changed her style. Little black frocks, that's what she's been going in for, and nothing to trim them with but a little string of pearls and a diamond brooch." She paused, and a tall cadaverous man in black velvet gown sprang up from the solicitor's bench. "I wonder who *he* is," whispered James, and the friendly constable leant over and explained: "That's the *Advocatus Diaboli*."

"Consider, madam," now thundered this functionary, pointing a lean finger at the witness. "Can you swear that in the period under question the applicant's wife never asked you to add to a black frock so much as a Peter Pan collar? Remember, madam, you are on oath."

But the witness remained unshaken. "Not even a Peter Pan collar," she maintained stoutly, and frustrated, the *Advocatus Diaboli* sat down again.

"I think we will take the constable's evidence now," said the magistrate to his clerk, and Madame Dixon left the box and was replaced by a bareheaded policeman.

"Acting upon instructions," this policeman now recited, in a sing-song voice, "I proceeded to the residence of the applicant in Fitzjohn's Avenue, NW3, and have for the past three months closely observed the movements of the applicant and his immediate family." Here he paused for breath and the magistrate, seemingly bent on cutting a long story short, observed, "I think you can spare us all the details. It will be sufficient if you simply answer my questions. What did you observe of the applicant's social habits?"

"During the period of my observation," replied the constable, "it was noticeable that neither the applicant nor his family mixed with any of the other residents of the neighbourhood, excepting only a Mr. Brownrigg who occupies the adjoining residence."

"Yes?" said the magistrate with interest, looking up from his notes. "Is anything known of this Mr. Brownrigg?" He glanced largely round the Court and a little man, clearly a solicitor, jumped up and said, "I think, sir, that you will find that Mr. Brownrigg's application for re-grading to A is down for hearing before you tomorrow."

"Thank you, Mr. Wiggs," said the magistrate. He turned to the witness again. "Have you anything to add to your statement?" he asked.

"It was noticeable," said the constable, "that on each occasion that the applicant and his wife proceeded to the West End together, it was invariably their practice to partake of food in AB restaurants only."

"Anything else of interest?" said the magistrate wearily.

The constable licked his finger and turned over the pages of his notebook. "It also seems," he said, "that applicant's children were removed from their schools at the beginning of the current term and placed under the charge of a resident governess."

"I think I have taken enough evidence," said the magistrate. "You may stand down." He turned to his clerk and said, "Recall the applicant."

James and Ughtred looked on with interest as a tall sturdily built man in a neat pin-stripe suit climbed into the witness box and steadfastly faced the magistrate, only the uneasy twitching of his fingers betraying his nervousness.

"Bartholomew Waddington," pronounced the magistrate. "I have listened carefully to the evidence on your application for re-grading to A, and I must say that it appears to be satisfactory. It seems that since you, by dexterous manipulation, accumulated a sum of money fit to be called a fortune, you and your wife have sincerely done your utmost to live in the ways and ape the manners of your betters. As you know, this court has itself no powers to bestow upon you the coveted designation of A; this can be done only by the High Court, and I am, therefore, granting your application for a certificate to lay your case before that august body."

The man in the box seemed overcome with emotion. In a broken voice he whispered, "Thank you, thank you, sir," and stumbled away, his face transfigured with happiness.

The magistrate said, "I will take the next case now."

Ughtred leant over to James and whispered, "Could you bear to hear another case? I must confess that I myself am quite enthralled."

"Well, let's just hear the next one," James whispered back and settled himself in his seat.

✿   ✿   ✿

There were sounds of disturbance and a feminine voice raised in sharp protest. James looked up and saw that someone was now standing in the hitherto empty dock. He gripped Ughtred's arm sharply and hissed, "Ughtred, look!" and Ughtred looked and then, in a voice charged with emotion, said, "God bless my soul, it's Janice."

And so it was. But a Janice how changed from the confident bewitching creature that James had last seen with the Governor-General on the promenade deck! Gone was the make-up that she used to apply with such consummate artistry. Gone the sleekly brushed blonde hair, the immaculate and obviously outrageously expensive garments. In their place stood a sullen girl with a face blotchy from tears, hair tousled and dull, clad in a shapeless garment of rusty black. And this was the creature for whom James had endured such spasms of jealous desire! He gazed on the wreck that had once been the glamorous Janice Brown with such a mixture of feelings that he found himself totally unable to sort them out.

The magistrate was saying: "What is the charge?" and was answered, "Not knowing her place."

"Dear me," said the magistrate, peering over his glasses. "How many more of these cases are we going to get? Well, I suppose I'd better take the evidence."

During the hearing of the evidence James's attention wandered. Somehow or other it seemed to him more important that he should elucidate his own emotions than listen to the statements which were, it seemed from the grave demeanour of the magistrate, piling up heavily against Janice Brown. Old desires die hard and even now, it seemed to James as he looked at Janice, there could be pleasure in taking this poor broken thing and making her his own. And would there perhaps be, in some odd uncomprehended way, an even greater pleasure? James couldn't be quite sure. Suddenly the taking of the evidence was over and James's emotions were still in as much of a tangle as ever.

He heard the magistrate ask: "Janice Brown, have you anything to say?"

At this Janice for the first time showed signs of animation and James's attention was caught by the scene before him. The magistrate repeated: "Have you anything you wish to say?" and Janice said sullenly, "I can't see that I've done anything wrong."

The magistrate sighed. "Janice Brown," he said, "you seem to be quite incapable of appreciating the gravity of your offence. I shall recapitulate in some detail in the hopes that this case may be reported in full and serve to deter other young women from the same offence. On your arrival in England you were, quite properly, registered as a C, since your occupation seemed to be clearly that of Accommodation Girl. You were presented with a little booklet setting out the limitations in the conduct of such female C's which you do not appear to have read. At all events, immediately on your arrival in London you attempted to enter the Mayfair Estate, which is absolutely forbidden to women of your grade unless accompanied by an A male, or under license, and it appears from the constable's evidence that only after creating a disturbance were you persuaded to spend the night with a girl friend in the Maida Vale area. The next day, by means as improper as they are horrifying, you prevailed upon the gatekeeper at the North Audley Street entrance to let you into the Mayfair Estate. Once in, you seem to have behaved with a total lack of decorum. Not only did you insult the hairdresser who refused to do your hair, the couturier who refused to make your clothes, and the beauty specialist who would not sell you a brand of cosmetics legally reserved for A's, but you then proceeded to walk into the lounge of a luxury hotel without having first applied for the special West End Hotel license for C Perambulants which, had you behaved differently, you might quite well have been granted. You do not appear to realize that times have changed and that the conditions in which ladies and pick-up girls were indistinguishable have gone forever. Only a very drastic sentence can match the gravity of your offence, and I therefore direct that you be degraded to the status of E now and hereafter. This means that your hopes of making a solid career by becoming the regular mistress of a Grade A male are frustrated. And I trust that this heavy sentence may serve as a deterrent in other cases of which, lately, there have been all too many."

He ceased and Janice was dragged struggling from

the dock. Then and then only, when it was too late, did James know what he had been feeling and he was possessed with a dark and overwhelming rage. The magistrate was already starting the next case. Ignoring Ughtred, James rose and strode to the door. "Will they let the last prisoner free straight away?" he asked, the constable answering, "Just as soon as they've given her her new disc, they will," and then, as James turned away, he added, "If you'd take a warning from me, sir — " but James was already striding across the hall.

Ughtred, trotting frantically behind him, caught him up as he reached the door. "James," he panted, clutching his arm and gasping from exhaustion, "James, I beg of you to consider. Surely you do not want to risk your career now, just when the future seems so rosy?"

James's wild rage died down and he stood for a moment irresolute. Ughtred, seeing this, pressed his advantage.

"James," he pleaded, "James — " but James, his moment of indecision over, was striding rapidly in the direction in which he supposed the prisoners' exit might be and Ughtred, unwilling to abandon him, scurried after.

He caught him up to find him questioning a policewoman of solid and unsympathetic demeanour. "Yes," she was saying, "the prisoner has already gone. No, she didn't say where she was going. As a matter of fact," she added with a malicious glint in her eye, "there was a young man waiting for her at this very door, and the two of them went off together."

"Thank you," said James dully. He didn't seem to know what to do next and meekly allowed Ughtred to take his arm and lead him away.

＊ ＊ ＊

In the pub whither he had taken James, Ughtred helped him to down a couple of stiff whiskies and then made up his mind.

"James," he said in a voice whose solemnity aroused James from his stupor and made him look up with a certain interest, "James, despite the disparity in our ages, you and I have long been good friends, have we not?"

"Oh, yes," agreed James, and took another gulp at his whisky.

"I know," continued Ughtred, "that nothing is more likely to strain friendship than the giving of unpalatable advice, but I am too fond of you, James, to refrain. James," he continued, a note of spontaneous fervour creeping into his voice, "think of the opportunities now opening before you and ask yourself whether it would not be an act of crass idiocy to cast them away for a degraded drab."

"This is pretty strong language, Ughtred," protested James. "I remember that on the island, you and Janice seemed to get on pretty well together."

"Circumstances alter cases," retorted Ughtred sententiously, "and today the circumstances are very greatly altered. Naturally at your age, you feel certain strong urges. But believe me, James, there are better ways of satisfying them than those that may well cost you your whole social position."

"I know all that," said James rudely, stung by certain assumptions in Ughtred's voice, "but I'm tired of casual pick-ups. A man gets lonely and I want something more — more permanent."

"Then why don't you get married?" suggested Ughtred gently.

"Don't want to," James muttered sulkily. "I want to have a good time of the sort you can't have when you're married — but I want someone to share it with."

"There are ways — " began Ughtred, and then stopped.

James grumbled, "Wish I knew what they were."

Ughtred came to a decision. "James," he said with gravity, "when I told you of the admirable arrangements made on my behalf by the Ministry of Social Security, I didn't tell you all. It did not seem to me proper to discuss certain aspects of my private life with a friend as young as yourself, and I hope you will believe me when I say that only the deep concern I feel for you impels me to break through my reticence."

James became sensible of increasing interest and his manner encouraged Ughtred to proceed.

"Though no doubt I seem to you quite elderly," he said, "you must appreciate that the urges of which we were speaking do not necessarily diminish in exact ratio to the advancing years. But in my own case I had long made up my mind that, although these existed, it would be impossible for me to do anything about them. I was fully conscious," he said sadly, "that my outward appearance was no longer so prepossessing that I could hope to be accommodated for my own sake; nor had I the financial wherewithal to proceed in the alternative manner."

"Pretty tough," muttered James, in an embarrassed voice.

"You must judge then," continued Ughtred, "of my delight when I found that the Ministry already had such cases as mine firmly in hand. I will spare you the details and, to cut a long story short, need only tell you that I am now fixed up with a buxom widow called Kitty who is always happy to receive me in her pleasant cottage in Park Village East which has been officially scheduled for such dwellings under the new Town and Country Planning Act."

"Whew!" whistled James, momentarily forgetting his manners in his astonishment at this revelation. And then he remembered them and said politely, "Well, I do congratulate you, Ughtred. I hope you'll be very happy."

"Thank you," said Ughtred, blushing a little. "I cannot deny that I was — well — pleased to find such arrangements were the usual thing again. Of course, in my father's day it was all taken for granted, but of late years — " he sighed, and then, recollecting himself, returned to the business in hand. "So you see, James," he said, "there is absolutely no need for you to marry or to burn. Just go along to the Ministry tomorrow and see what they can organize for you."

But James had turned sulky again. "It's Janice I want," he said obstinately. "I wanted her on the island and I want her now. And if the new régime can't fix *that* for me, well I don't think it's much better than the old one."

Chapter 8

IT IS, HOWEVER, a universal tendency of humanity to say things that they don't really mean, and despite his rude comment to Ughtred, James felt, as he tied his white tie in front of the glass, that the new régime had a great deal to be said for it. Crabtree had brought him up a cocktail to drink while he was dressing and he now finished this, gave a last brush to his hair, slipped on his jacket and was ready.

He met Rupert on the stairs, and asked, "Would you like a lift? I thought of taking the Lagonda."

"No, let's take a hansom," protested Rupert. "I always think that for an evening outing of this sort, they are so much more in keeping. We both go the same way, so we can quite well share one."

James readily agreed to this new proposal and Crabtree was sent off to find a cab.

"By the way, I hope you've remembered your white gloves," said Rupert, as they stood waiting on the doorstep. "One doesn't want to be pernickety, but after the laxity of the last few years, hostesses *are* very particular about everything being just so."

"By Jove, I'm glad you mentioned them," cried James, "I'm ashamed to say I never thought about it," and he turned to go upstairs.

"*And* a clean collar," shouted Rupert after him. "One's apt to need it before the evening's over," and when James came down again correctly equipped, he found the handsome cab waiting outside the door.

Never had James known such a sensation of pure pleasure as he now felt bowling to a party in a hansom cab. As they clip-clopped through the streets of London's West End, he felt all the years of disappointment and frustration, of making-do and then not making-out, of loss and the increasing certainty of failure, drop away. And in their place was left a feeling of assurance such as he had barely imagined, of certainty, of absolute security. Ahead of him he saw stretch years of fulfilment and pleasure, of idleness and delight. This was the life that his forebears had lived, the certainty on which they had depended. Tonight James, making his first entry into the glittering Society of the new régime, knew that he was entering upon his heritage.

Let us picture him, as he climbs from the cab and waves a cheerful "Au revoir" to Rupert outside Lady de Maltravers's mansion in Belgrave Square. Let us gaze on him as he climbs the red-carpeted steps under the gaily striped awning, a tall square-shouldered young man in faultless evening dress, his face bronzed from years of tropic sun, his demeanour an enviable blend of modesty and assurance. Let us applaud him, Disraeli's ideal young Englishman, as he goes into the gentlemen's cloak-room, deposits his hat, and emerges to meet the company.

❋　　❋　　❋

This was assembled in a large glittering drawing-room, some twenty young couples besides his hostess who now came forward to meet him, her dignified plumpness elegantly encased in embroidered satin, her curled grey hair surmounted by a glittering tiara.

"Ah, Mr. Leigh-Smith," she gushed with an apparent effusion of real pleasure as she came forward and took James's hand. "How good of you to come at such short notice. Everyone is longing to meet you and to hear all about your adventures in — now where did they say it was? Now, let me see, I wonder how many people you know already?

It didn't seem to James, as he took a cursory glance at the group drinking cocktails in the middle of the room, that he knew anyone at all. But this, he found, as his hostess led him from one to another, was a complete mistake. In fact he knew nearly everybody. There were old school friends whom he had last seen selling cars in Great Portland Street, vacuum cleaners in Hendon, and themselves in Shepherd's Market. There were girls he had known running hat shops or modelling for photographers or learning to be kennel maids or simply propping up the bar in the Antelope, Eton Terrace. Nor was it surprising, he reflected as he greeted them, that at first sight they had seemed like strangers, for the change wrought in them by admirable clothes, faultless grooming and an atmosphere of leisure and security would have been unbelievable to one who had not witnessed it.

At this point his reflections were suddenly interrupted by the sight of the most beautiful girl he had ever seen. There she stood, unconscious of his approach, tall and queenly, golden-haired and blue-eyed, with an air that, even among all these others, impressed with its assurance and dignity. And he was about to be introduced to this goddess. James's heart beat so furiously that he could scarce sustain it, and he felt that its thumping must be audible to all when at last his hostess led him up to her and pronounced "Mr. Leigh-Smith — Lady Penelope Bosworth."

"Penelope!" cried James and "James!" cried Penelope, and the two of them fell to ecstatic hand-shakings and incoherent greetings.

"I see," pronounced Lady de Maltravers, "that you two already know each other."

"Dinner is served m'lady," now announced the butler from the door, and Lady de Maltravers said graciously, "Lady Penelope is your dinner-partner, Mr. Leigh-Smith, so you will have plenty of opportunities for renewing your former acquaintance."

*   *   *

Throughout the ten-course dinner, relieved only by a *sorbet,* James felt his amazement increase. He remembered that in the past he had thought that Penelope might be quite a decent-looking girl if only someone had got some money to spend on her. But never had he imagined that the mere expenditure of money could effect such a transformation as he now beheld.

And not only his wonder but his admiration deepened as the meal progressed. Penelope, who on the island had scarcely dared to open her mouth and then only to express agreement with the prevailing opinion, now seemed to have become a past mistress at that sort of conversation that James most enjoyed. True, she did not herself say much; but the opportunities she deftly gave James for airing his own opinions or stating his own views were such as to convince him, by the time the fingerbowls were put on the table, that she was the most accomplished conversationalist he had ever met.

By tacit consent, neither of them discussed their past common experiences nor the miraculous metamorphosis that had been wrought in their lives. Each instinctively felt that the formality of this dinner party demanded a wholly formal response. But there was that in her eye as she spoke that made James determine, as the ladies left the table, that an opportunity for more intimate discussion must shortly be found.

*   *   *

"I say, James," said "Stinker" Warlock, an old school friend, as they went to the gentlemen's cloakroom together, "you certainly are a lucky dog."

"How d'you mean?" asked James.

"Mean to say you didn't know that Penelope Bosworth looks like being the catch of the season," said his old friend incredulously. "No, no, you can't come that one over old Stinker! And it certainly looks as if the interest isn't all one-sided."

James laughed deprecatingly, but Stinker's words had started a new train of thought in his mind. He had spoken truly when he had told Ughtred that he had no notion of marrying just yet. Plenty of time, he had thought, for that sort of thing, and by "that sort of thing" he had subconsciously meant what he had seen marriage mean to his contemporaries in the late "thirties" — the inefficiently converted bijou cottage in Chelsea, the dearth of servants, the casual meals that so quickly palled, and the help demanded with the washing-up. He had not envisaged marriage as a state graced by a goddess, as a life lived amid surroundings of spacious splendour, and now, as he suddenly realized that marriage under the new régime must mean just that, a very definite intention formed in his mind.

Let no one think that in this flood of new emotion James had already forgotten those aroused in him by the sight of Janice in the witness-box. He had not. But with the mental dexterity instinctive in his forebears, James found himself easily able to compartmentalize his two desires, that for Janice and that for Penelope. A man, he told himself, wants one sort of thing from a wife and another sort of thing from a mistress and by

God, he said to himself with exultant fury as he decorously followed Penelope into the Daimler, I'm going to have a bloody good shot at getting them both.

❖ ❖ ❖

The dance at which they quickly arrived differed from dances he had known before chiefly in being an occasion of enjoyment. The drinks were straight champagne and not an adulterated beverage called "cup"; the cold salmon and the lettuce on which it lay were in the correct ratio to each other; the ice creams were neapolitans, ample wedges of vanilla, strawberry or pistachio, and each wedge tasting noticeably different from the others. The floor was large and sufficiently polished, the dance band versatile to a degree. In the large conservatory, a dexterous arrangement of potted palms afforded sufficient privacy for sitting-out, without providing enough for indiscretion.

Even given all these delights, I doubt whether I myself would have enjoyed this dance. But James, rather a different type, did so to the top of his bent. "May I have the sixth — the ninth — the first extra," he was forever saying to pretty débutantes who blushed delightfully and scribbled their names in his little programme. And "May I have the supper dance?" he had said to Penelope, and this she had promised him.

The dowagers around the wall approved of James. "Such a *nice*-looking boy," they said to each other. "An old Derbyshire family, we believe," and none of them looked in the least askance as James took her particular charge into the conservatory to ply her with ices.

He had thought that he would barely be able to live through the time till the supper dance, but he soon found that he was enjoying himself so much that he was quite ready to take this evening as it came and savour each delight as it rose. He saw Rupert who had, it seemed, effectively coped with the problem of the dull Miss Stanton and now seemed wholly absorbed in the pretty little Daisy they had met in the park that morning. He saw, too, her sister, the dark Evelyn, sitting unwanted in a chair by the wall, and "That's the right way to treat intellectual women" he gloated.

At last it was time for the supper dance and James came to claim Penelope. She had just finished dancing with an officer in the Grenadier Guards and looked, he thought with a surge of pride, lovelier, more queenly than ever. She rested her hand lightly on his arm and, as the orchestra struck up, drifted away with him to the intoxicating melodious strains of a Viennese waltz.

And, while they danced, a great many things that they would each have found the utmost difficulty in saying were tacitly understood between them. We have each had a Great Sorrow, said their hearts, there is always some part of our souls that must ache in solitude and yearn; and yet, said their hearts, we have for each other a sympathy and a liking greater than we could have for anyone else. We are the same sort of people and we have been through the same sort of things. It is certain that we should be far happier together than we could possibly be apart.

Thus their hearts communed while their voices uttered those conventional banalities absolutely obligatory to this sort of occasion. "Jolly good floor," said James. "You going to the Eton and Harrow?" and Penelope, "We went to the Chelsea flower show — I do so love flowers" and then the music stopped and it was time for supper.

＊ ＊ ＊

They had no more opportunity for private conversation that evening. As the hours went by, the fun waxed faster and more furious, became increasingly communal and convivial and it was only at five o'clock in the morning, over the haddock Monte Carlo, that James found an instant to whisper to Penelope, "I shall call on your father tomorrow," and receive her willing blush of assent. Then he lost her in the security of chaperons collecting their charges and came home with Rupert in a hansom cab, tired and happy.

＊ ＊ ＊

James slept late next morning. For many years now he had been accustomed to early nights and up with the dawn, and his constitution had still to accustom itself to the many demands that would be made on it by his new profession. It was half-past ten before Rupert and he breakfasted together, and neither felt able to stand up to more than a piece of dry toast and a cup of strong coffee.

"What are you doing today, Rupert?" asked James as he leant back in his chair with a cigarette.

To James's immense surprise, Rupert turned a fiery red and looked down at the tablecloth. "This morning I've got an important call to pay," he said. "What are you doing, James?"

James, to his horror, felt himself flushing, too. "I've got an important call to make as well," he said awkwardly, and there was a moment's silence.

"I wonder," said Rupert carefully, "if your business is by any chance the same as mine?"

"It might be," said James cautiously. He waited a moment and then said, "You and Miss Marsham seemed to be getting on pretty well last night."

Impulsively Rupert leant forward, "I might as well make a clean breast of it," he said boyishly, "as you seem to have guessed in any case. Yes, Daisy and I fixed it all up in the conservatory and this morning I'm going to go and do the right thing with her papa." He smilingly accepted James's enthusiastic congratulations and then said, "And now, James — come clean."

"I thought you might have guessed," confessed James. "I'm going on the same errand as you — to see Penelope Bosworth's father."

The silence that followed his statement was overlong. At last he said belligerently, "Well! Aren't you going to congratulate me?"

But instead Rupert asked, "James, have you set your heart on this?"

"Certainly I have," answered James with a certain uneasiness. "And why not?"

Rupert said with a lukewarm attempt at heartiness, "Penelope's certainly a lovely girl. I wish you all the luck in the world."

"Why are you behaving so oddly?" demanded James. "Do you know something — is there any reason —?" he faltered and stopped.

Rupert said reluctantly, "Well, one hears things — I mean, I don't think you'll find it all that easy. But I certainly wish you luck."

❉   ❉   ❉

Rupert's manner had inevitably destroyed a measure of James's self-confidence, and the ebullience he had felt at the ball had wellnigh evaporated by the time he stood on the threshold of Penelope's home in Berkeley Square and asked to see Lord Starveleigh. "Will you please follow me, sir," said the butler, and led James into the study where Penelope's father, in frock coat and stock, sat reading the Herd Book of the Guernsey Cattle Society.

He looked up as James entered and waved him to a seat. "Well, Mr. Leigh-Smith," he said, "and what can I do for you?"

"Lord Starveleigh," said James with as much manly dignity as he could possibly muster up, "I wish to ask your permission to pay my addresses to your daughter."

"Hrrumph!" said the nobleman non-committantly. "Which one?"

"Penelope," said James, and waited.

Lord Starveleigh swung round in his chair and pulled at a crimson bell rope. "We can discuss this best over a glass of sherry," he said, and the two men sat in a silence that James did not feel was wholly hostile, until the sherry arrived.

"Young man," said Lord Starveleigh at last. "Had you approached me with this proposition before the new régime took over, you would have been as welcome as hay in March. Anyone who wished to marry any of my daughters would have been greeted by my wife and myself with open arms. But times have changed, young man. I'm only the primary producer; you've got to buy through the retailer."

"I don't quite understand," said James puzzled. "Who *is* the retailer in this case?"

"The Ministry of Social Security," said Lord Starveleigh. "It's all a part of this tendency towards centralization. I suppose it's a better idea on the whole. In the past, there were a hundred different ways of trying to get a daughter married, but none of them were altogether efficient. Now, at last, you're sure of picking from a really comprehensive list, and I'm told they've even got instant teleprinter communication with all the important county centres. It's to the Ministry of

Social Security you'll have to go, my boy, if you want to marry my daughter."

"I see," said James dully. He looked up to see a kindly gleam in Lord Starveleigh's eye. "I say, sir," he said impetuously, "what sort of a chance do you think I've got?"

Lord Starveleigh looked him up and down. "I wouldn't know," he said reluctantly. "I'm told the Ministry have all sorts of modern ways of making matches — psychological tests and whatnot that didn't exist in my young days. But I'll tell you honestly, my boy, I'd like you to marry Penelope. I used to know your father — he made me a packet once in Rand gold and I bought my best bull with it. I'd give you a chit to those fellows at the Ministry — but it would probably do more harm than good." He shook his head sadly, and James rose and prepared to take his leave.

"I'll tell you what, my boy," exclaimed Lord Starveleigh suddenly, "I'll give you a chance to do a bit of useful spadework on your own. We're having a house party at Starveleigh over the week-end; we've got an election coming off there next week so we want to put up a bit of a show. I'll get my wife to send you a card, and that will give you a chance to see a bit of the girl in her home surroundings. She's a good girl, though I say so." He shook James's hand heartily, and then sat down to the Guernsey Herd Book again.

❖   ❖   ❖

After a hurried lunch, James betook himself to the Ministry of Social Security in Curzon Street and asked for Mr. Featherstonehaugh. "He has not yet returned from luncheon, sir," said the pompous butler. "Would you like to wait, sir, or will you return later?"

"Not back from lunch!" repeated James in surprise. "Why, it's nearly three!"

"Mr. Featherstonehaugh seldom returns from his luncheon before a quarter to four," said the butler in dignified rebuke.

"Well, is there anyone else I could see?" demanded James.

"*None* of the gentlemen in the administrative grade," said the butler, still more haughtily, "return from their luncheons before half-past three at the earliest."

"Oh, all right then," said James sulkily. "I'll come back in half an hour or so," and he turned away.

For the next half-hour James pottered aimlessly round the streets of Mayfair. He passed a flower shop and thought to send Penelope a large bunch of red roses, rather vulgarly stuck about with maidenhair fern. He looked into a few antique shops and ordered a couple of very banal prints of Oxford to be sent to his rooms. He wandered in and out of Claridge's without, however, seeing anyone he knew, and finally ended up with a stiff brandy in Shepherd's Market, blessing the legislators who had seen fit to relax the rigours of the licensing laws for A's.

At last the time was up. James again rang the

Ministry bell and this time was shown into the waiting-room to wait, he was assured, only a very few minutes.

But the few minutes extended into a good quarter of an hour before James was once more shown up to Mr. Featherstonehaugh. This gentleman, looking as fully replete as gentlemen should after so long a lunch, greeted James cordially and asked him how he was making out.

"Extremely well," said James politely. "Everything seems to have been splendidly organized."

"We do our best," said Mr. Featherstonehaugh, "we do our best. And now, what can I do for you today?"

"Last time I was here," plunged James, "you spoke of a possible marriage."

"Yes," said Mr. Featherstonehaugh without inflexion.

"My views on the subject have somewhat changed," said James, plunging doggedly on. "In fact, I can fairly say that I'm definitely interested."

"Before you go any further," interrupted Mr. Featherstonehaugh, doodling on his pink blotting-paper, "I think I should tell you that when I casually mentioned the possibility of marriage to you, I had not expected that you would so quickly respond. As I told you at the time, you had chosen the profession that we wish, above all others, our youth to adopt. I think I can fairly say that we do our utmost to make it as attractive as possible. You must realize that it is hardly fair to us to desert it before we have had, if I may so express it, a fair return for our money."

"Why are you so keen about setting up Men-About-Town?" asked James curiously.

Mr. Featherstonehaugh leant forward eagerly. "It's to set the tone," he said earnestly. "You remember what Samuel Butler wrote: *The good swell is the creature towards which all nature has been groaning and travailing together until now. He is an ideal.*' If you think back over any other period of society when an aristocratic oligarchy was in power, you will realize that it was the swells — the Men-About-Town — who set the tone of that society. Unless your aristocratic young men are idle, extravagant and bent on pleasure, you cannot produce a hierarchial State based on the principles after which we strive."

He paused for breath, and James took the opportunity of saying, "You can't force me, can you?"

Mr. Featherstonehaugh fiddled with his paper knife. "Well — not yet," he said weakly. Then he brightened a little. "There's moral pressure, of course," he said.

"Not a spot of use," said James with decision. "If that's all you've got to say, I'll just pop off and marry Penelope."

"Penelope?" said Mr. Featherstonehaugh sharply. "Penelope who?"

"Lady Penelope Bosworth," said James, his hand on the door handle.

Mr. Featherstonehaugh made a wild dash for the door to intercept him. "Mr. Leigh-Smith," he panted, "please come back. Please sit down — please take a whisky. Now, supposing we just talk this little matter over like gentlemen."

James allowed himself to be led back into the room, settled in an armchair and provided with a glass of whisky. Then he asked, "Can I take it that you are now agreeable to my proposed match?"

"Mr. Leigh-Smith," said Mr. Featherstonehaugh leaning across his desk and speaking in a man-to-man sort of tone. "I will admit that perhaps I spoke a little hastily — I was disappointed and I fear I gave way to my disappointment. I was wrong. If you wish to marry, of course you shall marry. There's nothing more to be said."

"Good," commented James, and waited for Mr. Featherstonehaugh to get on to the subject of dowries and the like.

But Mr. Featherstonehaugh had picked up a thick wad of typewritten lists and was running his finger down it. "Let me see," he was muttering, "let me see. Ah, yes, now here's the very thing for you — Cotesdeveau, the Honourable Bridget; age: eighteen years; complexion: blonde; weight: ninety-six pounds; figure: svelte; interests: town life, clothes; other details — a most promising débutante although perhaps a trifle — " Mr. Featherstonehaugh abruptly stopped reading. "Well, are you interested?" he asked.

"No," said James.

"I can show you her photograph," pleaded Mr. Featherstonehaugh.

"No," said James again.

"Perhaps," suggested Mr. Featherstonehaugh hopefully, "you'd like a foreigner. I mean — having travelled and all that. I've only got to get through to our attaché — "

"No," said James very loudly. He stood up and faced Mr. Featherstonehaugh. "Why the hell — " he asked, "are you so keen I shouldn't marry Penelope Bosworth?"

Mr. Featherstonehaugh opened his mouth and then shut it again.

James said menacingly, "Come on. I want the truth."

Mr. Featherstonehaugh collapsed. He said, "We've got certain principles. We've made certain rules and we've got to abide by them, anyway at first. Later on, perhaps, we'll be able to be more flexible. But just now it's most important that people get into the right way of thinking."

"And what," asked James, "is there of wrong thinking in my wanting to marry Lady Penelope?"

"A great many things," returned Mr. Featherstonehaugh, gaining confidence. "For one thing, I gather you've fixed it all up yourself, simply by-passing this office without a moment's consideration. Now that won't do, Mr. Leigh-Smith. If you've got a government department set up to deal with things, it's simply striking a blow at the whole structure to deal with them yourself."

"What else?" asked James without comment.

"Then," said Mr. Featherstonehaugh, "it is the eventual function of Men-About-Town to marry débutantes. Whom else, indeed, should débutantes marry? You must realize that when this office first took over, we found a real bottleneck in unwanted female A's, and we're only just beginning to get it straightened out. And unless we can get each crop of débutantes married off as it comes out, we're only going to get the same pile-up all over again."

"What's that to do with me and Lady Penelope?" interposed James.

"Lady Penelope," said Mr. Featherstonehaugh, coughing discreetly, "is over thirty. Under any other régime than ours, she would simply have been marked down as past her market, and retired to the country. But we have done a great deal with her since her return. We have sunk a lot of money in her. You must remember that Lady Penelope springs from one of our oldest English families and is, therefore, a very marketable proposition. We have our plans for Lady Penelope and they are plans," he said firmly, "in which marriage to a lower-grade A, such as yourself, plays no part."

"Be damned to you," cried James rising and standing menacingly over the desk. "We're all as good as each other, aren't we?"

"Hardly," said Mr. Featherstonehaugh unperturbed, "since our whole society is founded on the assumption that we are not."

"But we are both A's!" cried James despairingly.

"There are grades within grades," said Mr. Featherstonehaugh smoothly, "and your continued inability to appreciate this would inevitably make us doubt whether we had correctly placed you to start with."

"Is — is that a threat?" said James, somewhat shaken.

"My dear fellow, no!" cried Mr. Featherstonehaugh. "What absolute nonsense. All I'm saying is, *if* you want to continue to enjoy your present position and income and all the rest of it — well, you'll just make up your mind to fall in with the Ministry's plans. After all, if we can only keep it up for a while, in quite a short time it will become instinctive in everyone and I doubt," he said with a little laugh, "if even we in the Ministry will be necessary then. Why, we shall just wither away."

He rose, and laying a friendly hand on James's shoulder, propelled him to the door. "Now, you just run along and enjoy yourself," he said kindly, "and next time you think of getting married, copy your friend Rupert and get a license from us before you propose."

Chapter 9

IT WOULD BE IDLE to deny that James was very considerably shaken by his interview with Mr. Featherstonehaugh. To be threatened is never pleasant, and the less so when the threat is likely to be effective. It seemed to James now that he faced trouble from every side; trouble if he traced Janice, trouble if he pursued Penelope. "Things have never gone right for me," he brooded morosely in his rooms; "at least," he said to himself, "under the old system, I could have had the pair of them and no questions asked," and sometimes he remembered that neither of them seemed to want him then and that he'd now got an income and a Lagonda, and sometimes he kidded himself that he could easily have had them both if he'd exerted himself, and what was the use of wealth and possessions without happiness? In short, he thought himself into a very doleful frame of mind, and when he heard Rupert come in, he locked himself in his room, unable to face up to the other's happiness.

But Rupert, who had guessed what had happened, was persistent as well as tactful and by dint of continued coaxing at last persuaded James to come out with him to a bachelor party in a friend's rooms. And the James who at last staggered home in the early hours having drunk too much champagne from too many chorus girls' shoes, was a James infinitely more sanguine and considerably reassured.

So when in the morning he received the invitation to the house party at Starveleigh Castle, he had no hesitation at all in writing a formal note of acceptance. "Everything is bound to come out all right in the end," he said to himself and he picked up the telephone and dialled Penelope's number.

"Oh! James," she said, and "Oh! Penelope," he said, and for a long time nothing more was exchanged than awkward incoherencies. But at last they each managed to convey to the other that their affections were unaltered and thereafter they talked with greater ease.

"By the way," said James, "this party your people have asked me to — I wondered if you'd like me to drive you down?"

"I'd love to," Penelope said, "if you could start early on Thursday, that is. I mean, if you haven't got a date for Thursday or anything."

"Nothing important," said James, ditching without reservation the little blonde chorine who had seemed so awfully keen on meeting him again. And then, after reiterated protestation of enduring affection, he rang off and finished his coffee.

He had decided to say nothing for the present about the Ministry's attitude. Talking, he believed firmly, always does more harm than good, and the less things were brought out into the open the better. Maybe, he thought optimistically, somehow or other — but at this point the telephone rang again.

It was Ughtred, who had also been invited to Starveleigh Castle, and had rung up to know if James was going, too. "Like to come with me in the car?" suggested James, and then cursed himself for breaking up his *tête-à-tête* with Penelope.

But Ughtred fortunately refused. "An open car," he said, "ceases to be a source of pure pleasure after a certain age, and that age I have long passed. But if," he added, "you would have the kindness to fetch me from my room and drive me to the station, I would be greatly obliged."

This James readily agreed to do, and then turned to meet Rupert who had also, it appeared, been invited with his Daisy to Starveleigh Castle and was driving her down in his own super-charged super-sports Bentley.

❖　　❖　　❖

And so on Thursday morning after an early breakfast, James drew up outside the back entrance to the Albany and, being an A, was, of course, allowed to leave the Lagonda in Vigo Street while he went in to fetch Ughtred, somewhat anxious to see the surroundings in which his friend now lived. These, he found, although not in any way his own cup of tea, were clearly just the right complement for such a character as Ughtred, from the sets of calf-bound books that lined the walls to the elderly gentleman's gentleman who was, it seemed, travelling down with his master.

Reader, look with pity on Ughtred Thicknesse as he leaves his chambers in Albany, thinking pleasantly of the welcome they will give him when he returns from his little holiday. For, though he knows it not, Ughtred Thicknesse will never enter those chambers again.

As it was, in blissful ignorance of this, Ughtred climbed happily into the seat beside James, while the gentleman's gentleman packed himself and the luggage in behind, and they all started off for Paddington station.

Ughtred turned to James. "I met Penelope at dinner last night for the first time since we landed," he remarked. "I would never have imagined it possible that she could be turned into the really remarkable beauty I saw."

"Yes, it is rather amazing, isn't it?" agreed James in the most non-committal voice he could manage. Ughtred looked at him sharply, but said nothing more, and eventually they pulled up at Paddington station.

*　　　*　　　*

"Well, James, it was most mannerly of you to act as my chauffeur," said Ughtred, after he had with difficulty extricated himself from the Lagonda and stood safely on the pavement. "I shall look forward to seeing you and Penelope again at dinner tonight."

"Oh! nonsense," said James cheerily, patting Ughtred on the back. "I'll see you onto your train first. I've got oceans of time."

"Then let us go first to the bookstall," said Ughtred. "I like to have a little reading r atter to while away a long journey."

"You've got your ticket?" James asked anxiously, but Ughtred replied, "I understand that I have no need of one; Lord Starveleigh has reserved a special Pullman coupé for such of his guests as are coming down by train."

"I wonder if the trains are as crowded as we heard?" mused James, and Ughtred said, "I really don't know, James. Perhaps Blenkinsop can tell us. Blenkinsop," he said, turning to his man. "What are travelling conditions like nowadays?"

"Under the admirable private ownership of the various companies," replied Blenkinsop with dignity, "anyone of any importance now finds them admirable. With all first-class carriages reserved solely for A's, there are always plenty of seats and no possibility of distasteful intruders. And with the old second class restored for B's and C's and the possibility of reserving seats in this class, there is really nothing to complain of."

"I suppose D's and E's travel third?" commented James, without much interest.

"Exactly, sir," agreed Blenkinsop.

"And what's it like in there?" asked James idly.

Blenkinsop's face now took on an expression of no slight hauteur. "You will excuse me, sir," he said icily. "I have not been sufficiently interested to ask."

Ughtred, seeing that James looked a little embarrassed at this exchange, now sent Blenkinsop off to deal with the luggage, and the two gentlemen walked on together to the bookstall.

"Yes, sir?" inquired the sharp-faced little man behind the bookstall counter, "what can I get for you, sir?"

"The *Spectator*, please," said Ughtred, and turning to James, added, "An admirably unbiased journal, I have always thought."

"No *Spectator*," interrupted the bookstall attendant.

"Perhaps a *New Statesman*?" suggested Ughtred. "I don't care much for its political views, but its book reviews are always good."

"No *New Statesman* neither," said the man. He leant over the counter. "You take my advice, sir," he said in a low voice, "and don't go about asking for that class of journal. It won't do you no good."

"But I don't understand," said Ughtred in a blank voice. "What has happened to these papers?"

"They've been suppressed," said the man.

"Suppressed!" repeated Ughtred. He looked, James thought, more white and shaken than he had ever seen him. "Do you mean that these papers have been suppressed by law?"

"Not exactly," said the man with a wicked grin.

"They was just told to shut down and shut down they did. It came out afterwards that the Government hadn't no legal authority for telling them to do so, but just the same, there wasn't a squawk out of none of them. Mind you, there's been laws passed since to make it all watertight and shipshape. Wouldn't hardly do for that class of journal to be on the bookstalls nowadays, would it?"

"Hardly," agreed James. Ughtred said nothing. Indeed, his face seemed oddly drawn and rigid and James, a little worried, took his arm. "Come on, Ughtred," he said gently, "or you'll miss your train, and that would never do, would it?"

Ughtred stared emptily round him. "My train?" he said, vacantly. "My train?"

James was getting really worried. "Don't you remember, Ughtred?" he said urgently, "you were going away for the week-end to Starveleigh Castle — to Penelope's people."

With a sudden jerk Ughtred seemed to pull himself together. "Yes, of course," he said hurriedly. "I was thinking of something else. Yes, of course. We have to catch a train."

"Come along then," said James, gently pulling him by the arm. He was greatly relieved to see Blenkinsop waiting for them by the coach door. "You'll be all right now, Ughtred, won't you?" he asked anxiously and Ughtred said apologetically, "Yes, of course, James. It was very good of you to come along," and climbed heavily into the coach. Through the window James saw him reach a seat and sink into it. There was nothing more he could do and, still feeling uneasy, he went away to pick up Penelope.

❋   ❋   ❋

It was a perfect day for driving into the West. There was a blue sky and a light breeze, and all along the roads the lilac and wistaria were in flower. James felt like singing as he whizzed out of London, the windscreen flat before him and Penelope snuggling into the seat at his side. I'm a man who likes simple pleasures, he thought, a swell car and a swell girl and nothing to do — it's not much to ask — yet God knows they were the last things I expected to have when I climbed down the gangplank. Then he started thinking of his inferior position on the island and Penelope — she had an inferior position, too, he reflected: how glad she must be that things have turned out the way they have. On an impulse he said, "Penny, how you must have hated those years on the island."

Penelope didn't answer for a minute, and when she did it seemed to James there was an odd note in her voice.

"No," she said, "no. I didn't hate them."

"Good God!" exclaimed James in astonishment. "Whyever not?"

Again there was this same inexplicable pause before she replied, "James, I'd rather not talk about the island, please. That was one life and this is another one, and somehow, I have a feeling it won't do any good to hark back."

"Oh! all right," said James, feeling rather offended. He'd been secretly looking forward to doing a spot of discreet gloating over the reversed fortunes of the party. But he was not able to be offended for long, for soon Penelope, with that social dexterity she had so suddenly acquired, asked him for a simple piece of information, and in supplying this at great length to her receptive ears James gradually recovered his good humour.

❊　　❊　　❊

They had some little difficulty in finding an A hotel for lunch. James had thought this would be easy and had made no inquiries beforehand, but the policeman whom he finally stopped and asked told him that the position with regard to A hotels was still very difficult. "When they first took the hotel census for grading," said the constable, "they found that nearly every hotel in the country was B or lower, and the few that weren't were run by A's who showed a rooted objection to becoming C's. They turfed some of 'em out, and put in C's instead, but even then they didn't get the hotels they want. Seems like keeping hotels is a lost art as far as the countryside is concerned. If you care about food, sir, you take my advice and try one of the C pubs; likely as not you'll get a good dish of cold meat and some bread and cheese."

So they took the constable's advice and made a very excellent and filling lunch off cold roast beef and stilton in a small market town. And this so mellowed them that by the time they took the road again they were planning quite amicably the life they'd have together, although, perhaps, one should admit that James did most of the planning while Penelope's function was chiefly to supply pleased noises of agreement.

"I thought we might get a large flat in town," said James, "and a place in the country for week-ends and things. I'd like to go winter-sporting in January and then to the south of France. Then we'd come back to town for the season and then we might take a yacht or something and go cruising around. Then we'd have a spot of shooting in Scotland and then we could hang around town till Christmas. We might have Christmas with your people," he put in kindly, "and then we'd start all over again."

"And how long would we go on doing it for?" asked Penelope with something of her old timidity in her voice.

"Why, indefinitely," said James, staring in surprise. "I mean, I can't think of anything better to do, can you?"

"I suppose not," said Penelope, and even to the unperceptive James it seemed that there was a sigh behind the words. He felt vaguely uncomfortable and for some miles they drove in silence.

It was in the outskirts of an ugly manufacturing town about thirty miles from Penelope's home that the car broke down. Let no one cast any aspersions on Lagondas; James had forgotten to put any water in, and really, it was a wonder that the car had gone as far as it had.

Now he said "Damn!" and stared at it gloomily. There is nothing a man dislikes more when he's out with a girl than an unintentional mechanical breakdown. "Damn!" he said. "I'll have to get some water from someone."

"Why not try this house?" suggested Penelope, and looking round, James saw the house outside which they had stopped. It was a neat little semi-detached suburban villa with a lot of imitation beams over its casement windows and a bar of rustic wood that read "Anona" hanging under the front porch. Behind the sitting-room curtains he saw a woman watching them. "Might as well have a shot," he said, and opened the little green-painted gate, tramped up the crazy-paving and rang the bell.

In a few moments he returned to the car, the woman behind him carrying the water in a chipped enamel jug. Her hands were red with work, her hair crisply curled in stiff waves, and from her tired face it was impossible to say what age between thirty and sixty she might be.

James managed to undo the radiator cap and poured

the water in. "She's boiling hot," he said gloomily as he listened to it sizzling. "We really ought to wait a bit and let her cool down."

"We don't want to be late for dinner," said Penelope anxiously. "They dine at half-past eight, and we've got to bath and change."

"It's just after half-past six," put in the woman timidly, picking up her jug from the pavement where James had left it.

"It won't take us more than another three-quarters of an hour, darling," said James, "and I really think we ought to give her a spot of time to cool down."

"Well," said Penelope, "if we must, we must."

The woman looked from one to the other and then said nervously, "Excuse me, but I wonder if you'd care to come in and wait in the house. It's ever so nice and cool, and you'll get that hot, sitting out there in the sun."

James thought there was good sense in what she said. But he didn't like to accept, not knowing what rules he might be infringing if he thus entered what was so clearly a B home.

Penelope saw his hesitation and leant towards him. "It's all right so long as we patronize her," she whispered. "It's only having a social relationship that's not allowed." She turned to the woman. "Thank you very much indeed," she said graciously. "That is a very kind thought of yours." She got out of the car and went up the little path, the woman standing aside to let her go.

* * * *

Mrs. Brown seemed quite delighted at receiving them in her home. She fussed them into the neat little siting-room with its wistaria cut-outs fringing the mottled beige walls and settled them into a large sofa covered with green cubistic material. She turned on the electric light in its carved amber bowl and tucked fringed satin cushions behind their backs. "There now," she said. "Now if you're quite comfy, I'll just bring you in a cup of tea. My hubby always likes a cup of tea the minute he gets in. There's nothing like a cup of tea, he says, after a hot day."

She bustled out of the sitting-room, leaving James and Penelope silent on the sofa, staring stiffly at the brown-stained mantelpiece where stood a square-faced clock, a nude bronze girl, and a turquoise-blue china dog. Very soon Mrs. Brown was back with the nice cups of tea and an appetizing plate of biscuits neatly spread on a black and chromium tray. She set the tray on a little ironwork-and-glass table beside them and herself sat down in the opposite armchair.

"I do hope you'll like my biscuits," she said with pathetic eagerness. "I don't suppose they're quite what you're accustomed to, but my hubby — I just can't keep him off them."

"They're delicious," said Penelope kindly, "but we

mustn't eat too many of them, or there won't be any left for your husband."

"Oh! that's quite all right," Mrs. Brown insisted. "You just go ahead and eat as many as you want. I can easily bake up a fresh batch before Mr. Brown comes back from work."

"What time do you expect him?" asked James casually, stuffing his mouth with the biscuits, which were indeed excellent.

Mrs. Brown sighed. "I doubt he'll be back before midnight, today being market day," she said, "but usually he's home about ten."

"What's his work?" inquired James without much interest.

"He's a grocer," said Mrs. Brown, and pushed the biscuits again towards Penelope.

But Penelope and James were looking at each other in amazement. "A grocer!" repeated James at last, "But whatever does he find to do till such ungodly hours? Does he have a lot of forms to fill up or something?"

"Oh! no," said Mrs. Brown, apparently surprised at their ignorance. "There's no more forms for B's, I'm glad to say. But since we went back to private enterprise, there's been no more statutory closing hours either. The Government said it wasn't fair to stop hardworking men of initiative from making their fortunes if they wanted to."

"I see," said James with a little laugh. "I take it your husband is out to make his fortune."

"That he isn't," contradicted Mrs. Brown with spirit. "We don't want any fortune. We were quite happy shutting at five-thirty P.M. with a half-day Wednesdays and we made quite enough to live the way we wanted to live."

"Then why does Mr. Brown work so hard now?" asked Penelope.

"Well, we don't want to be ruined, do we?" said Mrs. Brown, staring. "And if the big store opposite stays open till all hours, what else can hubby do? Of course, *they've* got plenty of assistants working shifts and hubby's on his own. But if he didn't stay open as late as they did — why, all his customers would go elsewhere."

"Would they?" asked Penelope.

"Of course they would," said Mrs. Brown. "People like to shop where people will put themselves out to serve them. I do myself. Well, it's free enterprise, I'm told, and we mustn't grumble, only I must say it sometimes worries me, hubby working so hard and nothing to show at the end of it."

"So he isn't making his fortune?" commented James.

"Course not," said Mrs. Brown indignantly. "That stands to reason. If one stays open late, then all the rest must, or go under, and you're just where you were before, only more overworked."

"So you don't altogether like life under the new régime," said Penelope with something of a sigh in her voice.

Mrs. Brown immediately looked scared. "Now, I never said that," she said uneasily, "And there's no call to go saying I did. As a matter of fact I like it very much, and all the other B housewives say the same."

"Why?" asked Penelope.

"I'd be pleased to live under any régime," said Mrs. Brown, "that could do away with queueing and give me help in the house — and that's just what this one's done."

"How did it do that?" asked Penelope and James simultaneously.

"My, you two don't seem to know much about the way things have gone," said Mrs. Brown with a little laugh. "Anybody'd think you were foreigners. Of course there's no one queueing with all the shops open till all hours and being able to go shopping just when it's most convenient to you. And it's not as if anything was in short supply. There's plenty of goods in all the B ranges, though I must admit the quality and the variety aren't nothing to write home about."

"But what about the help in the house?" asked Penelope with real interest.

"Oh! that was easy," answered Mrs. Brown, "ever since they reintroduced piecework for D's and then cut the rates. D's can't hardly make both ends meet nowadays, not without someone in the family goes out to service, just like they used to in the old days."

James commented: "So B's have D servants?"

"Well, that's only natural, isn't it?" agreed Mrs.

Brown, "and I must say I've no complaints, nor have any of my neighbours. We B housewives 'ud put up with any kind of a régime so long as it gave us help in the house."

"I can understand that," said Penelope. She rose and shook the biscuit crumbs from her skirt. "I think the car will have cooled down by now," she said to James, and then turned to Mrs. Brown and held out her hand.

"Good-bye," she said graciously. "It was *most* kind of you to invite us into your nice little home, and the biscuits were really excellent."

"It was a pleasure," said Mrs. Brown earnestly, and shook both their hands. James said, "Good-bye, Mrs. Brown, I think your husband is a very lucky man."

❧   ❧   ❧

Back in the car, Penelope said, "I suppose that's the sort of home I'd have lived in if — " she broke off suddenly.

"If what, darling?" asked James tenderly.

"Oh! nothing," said Penelope, and in silence they sped over the roads until they reached Starveleigh Castle.

Chapter 10

THERE IT IS," said Penelope at last, and James swung the car round and came to a stop before the closed iron gates.

He was really most impressed. These tall stone pillars topped by heraldic griffons, the long shady drive stretching into the distance as far as the eye could see, the neat little ivy-clad octagonal lodge beside the road —all these combined to make a picture on which James's eye could rest with the utmost content. "Nobody and nothing is to stop me from marrying Penelope," he vowed to himself, and then he turned to her and said, "Well, darling, what do we do next?"

"Blow your horn," said Penelope, and so James blew his melodious French horn, and a rosy-cheeked woman with four little children clinging to her apron came out of the lodge. She pulled open the gates, and then stood aside to let the car through, both she and the children bobbing curtseys as it passed them. "God bless their pretty faces," she said in an audible aside, and James increased his speed and bowled on down the smooth surface of the drive.

On and on they went under the shady chestnut trees, past herds of fallow-deer browsing in the sunlight, past little streams rippling between shaven banks, past gamekeepers in brown corduroys with guns under their arms and each as winsome as any Lady Chatterly could wish. "What a beautiful place it is!" said James in amazement, "and how splendidly it is all kept up!" and Penelope replied, "It's quite incredible to me, the difference in the place. When I went away, it was so dillapidated, you'd have thought nothing could ever have put it right." "Have you got any brothers?" asked James with apparent irrelevance, and Penelope said, "No, why?" "Oh! nothing," said James, "I just wondered," and inwardly determined again that no one and nothing should be allowed to thwart his desires.

At last they crossed the dark translucent moat and drew up before the castle itself. James stared about him in wondering amazement. Before him he saw the Norman entrance gate, barred by its ancient portcullis. To his right stretched a long, low Tudor wing, its leaded windows heavy with floral and heraldic emblems and beside it what was clearly a Regency orangery; the wing to his left had patently been started in late-Gothic times and finished in Balmoral. In short, it was a superb and wholly British piece of pure sharawaggi. This James didn't know; "My God, it's magnificent!" he breathed as he climbed out of the car and watched the liveried footmen come forward and disembarrass it of its luggage.

"Don't bother with the car," said Penelope, "they'll put it away for you," and so James left the footmen to it and followed her into the entrance hall.

There they were greeted by the old butler whose maudlin eye said more clearly than words that he had once dandled Penelope on his knee. "The company have gone up to dress," he explained in a quavering voice, and then turning to James, "I have ordered a cocktail to be sent up to your room, sir."

"Nothing could be more welcome," said James heartily, and the old butler went on, "You are, of course, in the Bachelors' Wing, sir. Edward will show you to your room. Edward!" he called, and a stalwart young footman came forward. "I do hope you'll be comfortable, darling," said Penelope in an undertone and James replied, "I'm sure I shall, dearest," and then, in a still lower tone, "I'll be counting the minutes till I see you again." For a moment he held her hand in a lingering clasp and then they parted, the old butler and his minions looking benignly on.

*   *   *

The Bachelors' Wing was situated in the Balmoral portion of the castle, and here the footman led James and deposited him in a sufficiently comfortable bedroom that had a little card with his name on it neatly inserted in a slot on the door. Short as had been the time since his arrival, his evening clothes were already tidily laid out, and the promised cocktail was waiting on a silver salver. James hurriedly dressed himself and was just wondering how in the world he could possibly find his way back to the hall again when there was a knock at the door and Rupert entered.

"So you got here safely, old boy," he greeted James.

"We were beginning to get a bit worried about you. I said for a joke that you and Penelope had probably rushed off to Gretna Green and got married, and old Featherstonehaugh turned so white I thought he was going to faint."

"What! Is Featherstonehaugh here?" exclaimed James in some alarm; he did not relish the notion of pursuing his illicit suit under the gaze of that cold official eye.

"He's quite well connected," said Rupert soothingly, for he mistook the cause of James's perturbation, "and, anyway, we're such a big party that you won't have to talk to him unless you want to. Incidentally, there's another chap here who says he knows you — a middle-aged type called Hardiman."

"Really," said James in surprise. "He's quite a nice bloke. I wonder what he's doing here."

"I believe Lord Starveleigh asked him down to address the electors on India," Rupert replied. "We're all expected to pull our weight, you know."

"But I'm no good at all at talking," protested James. "I wouldn't know what to say."

"They'll find some niche for you, no doubt," said Rupert airily. "Come along — time for grub."

There were at least forty people dining at Starveleigh Castle that night, though only half were actually members of the house party; the rest were local bigwigs, from the Duke who had driven over from his near-by residence to the village parson and his wife who sat uneasily near the foot of the table and listened deferentially to their betters. James found himself seated about halfway down, next to Rupert's Daisy, whose easy flow of conversation kept him in merry humour through the long meal. Opposite him sat Penelope, who seemed to be talking to Ughtred with an earnest interest that occasionally gave James twinges of barely comprehended jealousy.

The food was majestic rather than excellent, the roasted peacock that formed the *pièce de résistance* being just the teeniest weeniest bit too tough for real enjoyment. The wines, however, were superb, from the excellent sherry they drank with the soup, right through the hocks and clarets that succeeded it, to the champagne that accompanied the elaborate ice pudding, a representation of the Houses of Parliament that cut to reveal bunches of late primroses that were immediately collected and handed to the lady guests on silver salvers. "What a charming idea!" said James admiringly to one of Penelope's sisters who sat on his other hand, and she replied, "Yes, we think very highly of Chef; he's had a special training in ceremonial dishes."

At last the long meal was over. The ladies had retired, the gentlemen had pulled up their chairs, and the port was circulating round the table. Rupert was now sitting next to James who whispered, "I say, Rupert — which is the candidate?" "That one," whispered Rupert, pointing out a dandified young man of about twenty-one who sat near Lord Starveleigh. "He doesn't look very *bright*," whispered James dubiously. "He's not," said Rupert, "but he's the Duke's third son."

Mr. Hardiman now leant across the table and said to James, "I suppose this is your first election since you got home. Must be very interesting for you."

"Most," said James untruthfully, for the machinery of politics interested him not at all. But Ughtred, who was listening, said, "I must confess I think it a piece of extraordinary good fortune to be at Starveleigh just now. Has the electoral process been changed in any way since we were last in England?"

He had spoken during a lull in the conversation and it was Lord Starveleigh who answered him. "Basically," he said, "it hasn't been altered at all, of course. The English electoral process isn't a thing one would care to meddle with. Of course, we've had to cut away a lot of dead wood."

"Hear, hear," said several of the gentlemen around him in well-bred voices.

"The position of the Opposition is then unchanged?" pursued Ughtred.

"Substantially," said Lord Starveleigh. "The liberals are now so accustomed to that position and have so well adapted themselves to it that it seemed good sense to let them continue. And since everyone takes it for granted that they'll never get in, hardly anyone bothers to vote for them. The whole thing is really on a thoroughly satisfactory basis now."

"And what about the Labour Party?" asked James with a real interest in the answer to this one.

There was a silence that even the insensitive James regarded as a shocked one. One or two gentlemen said, "Really!" in outraged undertones, and a little way away Mr. Featherstonehaugh was seen to be sadly shaking his head.

At last Lord Starveleigh said in an embarrassed voice, "Of course you've been out of England, Mr. Leigh-Smith. I think, gentlemen," he went on, looking round the table, "it would be only proper to answer Mr. Leigh-Smith's question, though he will readily understand that this is not, generally speaking, a subject we care to touch on. Perhaps, Mr. Brandon — " he asked questioningly, and a tall burly man took up the thread.

"I'm the agent for this election," he began, "and so perhaps I'm the best person to answer your question, Mr. Leigh-Smith, and the answer is that since we repealed the Reform Bill, there hasn't been a Labour Party. There couldn't be. There's no one left to vote for it."

"I see," said James, covered with shame and not daring to say a word more, though he didn't really see at all. But Ughtred filled the gap by saying, "I must apologize for continuing with the subject, since it appears to cause some embarrassment. But my history is not all it might be, and I must confess that I am not at all sure what the repeal of the Reform Bill would have entailed."

"Well," said Mr. Brandon in a far more courteous tone than he had used when speaking to James, "for one thing, it entailed a complete redistribution of seats in accordance with the conditions existing before 1832. We got the Boundaries Commission onto that, and really, they did a most satisfactory job. Manchester, for example, returns no member now, while our host here" — he bowed gracefully to Lord Starveleigh — "owns two. One is returned automatically by a gazebo in the garden while the other — that for the town of Starveham — will be elected on Saturday."

"You seem very sure of the electors," said Ughtred musingly.

"We may well be," returned Mr. Brandon. "With the present restricted electorate, hardly anyone is likely to vote other than Tory."

Ughtred commented. "So there's no more universal suffrage?"

"Only in the City of Westminster," explained Mr. Brandon. "And there they had it even before 1832. For the rest, the privilege of voting is confined, as it used to be, to men of property and a few very special classes, virtually all of whom are safe C's."

"Then why," asked James, unable to restrain himself any longer, "do you want us all to talk and canvass and so on?"

"Why, for the fun of it!" cried Mr. Brandon, and the other gentlemen applauded loudly. "There's nothing like a good old English election, as you'll see for yourself. What with the hustings and the rosettes and the free fights and the free beer — why, it's wonderful."

At this, a babble of enthusiastic agreement broke out and the conversation disintegrated into little groups, excitedly recalling the pleasures of the last election or presaging the joys of this. Rupert took advantage of this to lean over to James and whisper, "I ought to have warned you not to mention the Labour Party. It's thought to be very bad form to mention it."

"Well, I wasn't to know," said James in an aggrieved voice, "and anyway, I still don't understand. Surely all those working-class blokes who got the vote feel rather bad about it being taken away."

Rupert said sardonically, "The assumption is that they don't. And in any case, they've got plenty of voting to do. All the municipal elections, for instance, are in the hands of the B's, and really, they're much better at local affairs than they ever were at national ones."

"But the working-class types?" pursued James doggedly.

"They're all right," said Rupert airily. "They vote in the Trade Unions, for instance, and that keeps them going. And then, you know, the one thing they really wanted was a share in Works Management and they've got that now — Partnership in Industry, I believe they call it. Of course, they've got nothing to do with policy, but all the little things, like who brings round the cups of tea and what time they have it, they decide for themselves. And I believe it takes an awful lot of voting to decide it all, too."

"Are they quite content with that?" James asked incredulously.

"Most of them," said Rupert. "You know, everyone likes to think that the disputes within their scope are the most important in the world. What the new régime has done is to restrict everyone's outlook to the things they're fitted to deal with and, as you've seen, it works splendidly."

"Yes," agreed James with rather mixed feelings, and at that moment Lord Starveleigh rose from the table and said, "Well, gentlemen, I think we had better join the ladies. If you will all assemble in the Hall tomorrow at ten o'clock Mr. Brandon will give us all our instructions before we depart for Starveham."

❋   ❋   ❋

In the drawing-room the ladies were looking at picture books. Penelope had kept a vacant place on the sofa beside her and now smiled at James to join her. With Mr. Featherstonehaugh's eye upon him, however, James felt inhibited and self-conscious. "I do hope the drive down didn't tire you too much," said Penelope anxiously, feeling that something was wrong, and James clutched eagerly at this straw and pretended that only fatigue had dulled his ardour.

Lady Starveleigh, a negligible matron in black, said

suddenly, "Now we must have some music. Has any-one brought their music?"

There was a certain amount of pushing and shoving, but no one answered, and Lady Starveleigh, looking round, said, "What about you, Mr. Leigh-Smith? Have you any new ballads for us?"

James blushed a fiery red and said, "Oh! no, I couldn't possibly," and then, with desperate wicked-ness, "but I'm sure Mr. Featherstonehaugh would oblige."

But his shot misfired. Pressed, Mr. Featherstone-haugh readily admitted that he had, quite by chance, brought his music with him, and for the next half-hour James was compelled to listen to Mr. Featherstone-haugh rendering Gilbert and Sullivan with a facial ex-pression quite intolerable in its archness.

❋   ❋   ❋

James wanted to talk to Ughtred. Ughtred was, he knew, very fond of Penelope, and also seemed to be very well thought of in all the quarters that mattered. With this end in view he went, as soon as the company retired, to the bedroom with Ughtred's name on it, and, knocking, asked to come in.

But Ughtred, strangely, was not responsive. "I'm sorry, James," he said, looking, James thought, pitiably withered and haggard, "I don't feel like talking. At least, not tonight. I've got a lot of things I want to think about."

"Oh! all right," said James, affronted, and he was just going off to his own room, when a manservant appeared in the corridor.

"Mr. Leigh-Smith?" he said questioningly, and then, "You are wanted on the telephone, sir. A trunk call."

"Where is the telephone?" demanded James. He was rather worried. Who the devil could have possibly rung him up?

"If you will follow me, sir," said the servant, and led James downstairs to a dark little room full of ledgers and account books where an old candlestick phone stood waiting on the desk with its receiver off. The servant discreetly closed the door and left James alone.

"James, it's Rodney," said an agitated voice at the other end. "I had the most awful job finding you. At last I thought of getting through to the Ministry and, of course, they knew where you were."

"Whyever — " began James, none too pleased at the information that the Ministry was keeping track of his whereabouts.

"James," went on the voice, "something dreadful has happened. Joyce has run away and married her chicken farmer."

"Good God!" said James, appalled.

"And that's not all," said his brother. "Father and mother have definitely decided to apply for re-grading as B's. They say that if they tell the magistrate about their real tastes, there won't be any trouble about it at all."

"But what are we going to do?" broke from James.

"That's just the question," said Rodney despairingly. "I'd just made up my mind to accept the Derbyshire offer — but if father and mother turn B, I don't know if it will still hold good. Besides, what will you do?"

"It's damnable," said James angrily. "They don't seem to have any consideration at all. I was just thinking of contracting a very important marriage — " he stopped, remembering all the difficulties that stood in his way already.

"Look here!" said Rodney eagerly. "That might be the very thing. I think I can persuade the parents to hold their hands for a few days and give out that Joyce has gone to stay with relations or something. Then if, in the meantime, you can bring off a really sound engagement and get it into the papers — and if I write and accept the Derbyshire offer — well then, I mean, you and I have shown pretty clearly where we really stand, and we might even manage to get their application for re-grading turned down."

James said slowly, "I think maybe you've got something there."

"After all," pleaded Rodney, "we'd only be acting for their good."

"Certainly," said James unctuously. He thought hurriedly and said, "You can rely on me to do everything I can do to save the situation. You hold the parents off for a day or two, and I'll give you a ring on Sunday and let you know how things are going."

"O.K." said Rodney gratefully, and rung off. He'd never been one, James reflected, for acting on his own. Although the elder brother, he'd always relied on James to bring off any little plot or strategy that might be necessary. "And, by God," said James savagely, as he stood there shaking with fury, "I'll bring this off or bust."

Chapter 11

AFTER TOSSING uncomfortably all night, James was by no means pleased to be woken next morning at eight o'clock by a manservant with a cup of tea. "Prayers are at eight-thirty in the Great Hall," he said as he moved about the room, efficiently laying out James's clothes. "Am I expected to go to prayers?" demanded James in an outraged voice, and the manservant replied smoothly, "All the guests are expected to attend morning prayers, sir."

So, cursing under his breath, James dressed himself and followed the other guests to the Great Hall where rows of chairs had been placed in readiness. When the guests were all in their places, the servants filed in, rows and rows of them, and stood decorously at the back. A young man in a dog collar, described to James in a whisper as Lord Starveleigh's private chaplain, conducted the service which James, who was now feeling extremely peckish, thought intolerably long-winded. At last it was over. The servants filed out again and the guests were free to proceed to the breakfast room.

On the way James remarked to Rupert, "I didn't know the Starveleigh's were such a religious family."

"Oh, they're not," said Rupert, "but, you see, religion is one of the cornerstones of the new régime. They're hoping to make it obligatory for all A's and even B's to have family prayers every morning, while C's and D's will at least have to have readings from the Bible."

"What's the idea?" inquired James distastefully, for he was very much against compulsory religion since he had been to school.

"Haven't the foggiest," said Rupert without interest. "I suppose it's moral rearmament or something like that."

Mr. Featherstonehaugh, who was walking behind them heard this. He snapped, "It's nothing of the sort; people's morals are nothing to us, so long as they're discreet about them. The reason for our religious revival is to keep firmly before the minds of everyone a sound hierarchical vision." With this, he shut his mouth tightly again, and swept ahead of them into the breakfast room.

When a decent interval after breakfast had elapsed, the guests again assembled in the Great Hall, where they found Mr. Brandon waiting for them on a sort of improvised rostrum.

"Gentlemen!" he began. "I thought it would be a good idea to have a word with you all, to make sure that everything is fixed up and that everyone knows what they've got to do before we get to Starveham. First, about transport. A landau drawn by greys has, of course, been provided for Lord Topham, our candidate." Here he stopped and bowed clumsily in the direction of Lord Topham who tried to twirl a too-small moustache with an air of unconcern. "And if our

host's charming daughter, Lady Penelope, together
with Miss Daisy Marsham can be persuaded to take
their seats with him, I think we'll be able to present a
bevy of beauty with which the Whigs won't be able
to compete." Here there was a little desultory cheer-
ing. "Those of you who have your own carriages or
motor cars are requested to use them; you will find that
the staff have spared no pains to make them look as
attractive as possible. For the rest, a fleet of shooting-
brakes are waiting in the front drive."

"Now, I just want to check up on a few details,"
shouted Mr. Brandon. "The free beer has been laid on
— I saw to that myself. Sir Alastair, I think you were
going to arrange about the pugilists?" He looked in-
quiringly at a middle-aged man in a canary-yellow
waistcoat who removed his cigar from his mouth to
say, "It's all fixed," and then put it back again.

"Good," commented Mr. Brandon. "I think we can
rest assured that our friend Sir Alastair will have pro-
cured us a tougher band of bravos than any the Whigs
can muster. Now, what about the money?" He paused,
and Lord Starveleigh answered, "I've got it here. The
Paymaster-General sent down three bags yesterday."

"Then I think," said Mr. Brandon, "that we're all
set. It only remains for me to tell each of you what
you've got to do." He pulled a typewritten list out of
his pocket and James began to listen with close attention.

Penelope and Daisy, he discovered, were billed on

arrival to stand by the hustings and kiss every male voter who promised to support the Tory cause. Ughtred was to be in charge of the distribution of free beer. Mr. Hardiman was to be available in the Committee Rooms. Mr. Featherstonehaugh was given some strange job that sounded like "palm-greasing" and to James himself, together with Rupert Crooke-Haughton, was assigned the indeterminate function of canvassing. The company then began to shuffle out of the hall and towards the waiting transport.

"Suppose I came along with you in the Lagonda?" suggested Rupert to James. "Then we could have a bit of a chinwag en route about how we're going to tackle the problem."

"I wish you would," said James gratefully. "I really haven't the faintest notion of how to begin," and they both ducked their heads to avoid the pendant portcullis and came out on to the drive.

❀   ❀   ❀

James hardly recognized his car under the frouhaha of rosettes, ribbons and slogans with which the zealous servants of Lord Starveleigh had bedecked it. Eventually he managed to clear a way in for himself and Rupert, and swung the car down the drive and out of the gates.

"Tell me," he said to Rupert as they bowled along. "Whom exactly have we got to canvass? I thought that everyone who'd got the vote was a safe Tory anyway."

"Oh! we don't touch *those*," said Rupert, "the people we've got to canvass are the working-classes. You and I have been assigned some of the meanest streets in Starveham."

"But I don't see why," said James, greatly puzzled. "I mean, if they don't vote — "

"Plenty of good reasons," said Rupert cheerfully. "For one thing, they like it. There's quite an art, you know, in keeping the D's contented, and canvassing is definitely one of them. It gives them quite a kick to have an A walk in and say how clean it all is and kiss the baby."

"I'm damned if I'm going to kiss any babies," James protested forcefully.

"You'll come to it," said Rupert brightly. "Election fever does the strangest things to all of us. Then, of course, you have to persuade the man of the house to come along to the hustings and shout for Topham. It all helps."

"But surely," said James, "the man won't be home at this hour on a weekday — "

"Most of 'em will," said Rupert briefly. He went on: "And there's one thing I'd better warn you about. It's no good knocking or asking to come in, because sometimes some of the D's are inclined to be a little bit — well, funny. The best thing is to walk in and take it for granted you're welcome."

"I see," said James. "Thanks for the tip." They were running into the outskirts of Starveham now. Here were no bright suburban villas, no gay little modern houses, only row after row of sooted brick back-to-backs, topped with a uniform and depressing slate, and broken only by an occasional chapel or fish-and-chip shop.

"Lousy place, isn't it?" commented Rupert. "Topham must be thanking his stars he's only got to come here once every five years. What do you say we go along to the hustings and see a bit of fun before we start work?"

James readily agreed, and under Rupert's directions he steered the car through a maze of mean streets until they saw an open space ahead of them. Then they left the car and proceeded on foot.

❖   ❖   ❖

The market square seemed to be overflowing with a seething, shouting, exuberant *mêlée* of people. Over their heads, somewhere in the middle, James could dimly see two wooden structures on each of which stood a man. "There are the hustings," said Rupert, "come on!" and followed by James he elbowed his way through the crowds.

The first husting they came to was decked with shabby yellow bunting. "That's the Whig candidate," explained Rupert. "Shall we listen to him for a bit?" But "listen" was a misnomer, for the little grey-haired man was completely inaudible above the shouts, boos and cat-calls that proceeded from what seemed to be an organized group of rowdies all wearing blue rosettes.

At one moment, a member of the audience was seen to clap his hands and shout "Hear, hear," but he never spoke again for as he opened his mouth an enormous man punched him under the chin and he slid rapidly to the ground. "That's Billy Mason, the cruiser-weight champion of England," whispered Rupert respectfully, "we were lucky to get him." At this moment, the organized group suddenly loosed on the candidate a fusilade of cabbage stalks, tomatoes and rotten eggs. The last James saw of him, he was trying desperately to dodge these missiles, but the chances of anyone at all hearing anything he had to say seemed negligible.

"We'll just have a quick look at our own chaps," said Rupert, and they edged their way through the crowd again until they came to the Tory husting.

They didn't like to go too near in case Mr. Brandon should spot them and ask why they weren't on the job. But James managed to get a quick glimpse of Penelope in a large picture hat kissing a burly workman, and near her he saw Mr. Featherstonehaugh carrying a neat canvas bag into which he periodically dipped his hand and then pressed something into those of the bystanders. A strong smell of beer indicated that Ughtred must be performing somewhere near, but James didn't have time to seek him out, for Rupert tapped him on the arm and said, "Come on, we'd better get cracking."

*　　*　　*

They proceeded with some difficulty through the crowded streets. At one point they passed a loudspeaker van pressing slowly forward and booming "Support the Tory Party, the patron of Trade Unionism. Support the Tory candidate, the friend of the Working-Classes." As it passed them, they saw that it was being driven by the sporting Sir Alastair, who waved a cheery hand at them and shouted, "Good hunting!" as they passed. They went still further and as they went the crowds thinned out until at last they stood at the inter-section of two drab, grey streets and not a soul in sight.

"Well, here we are," said Rupert. "On your right, Commercial Street, which is my terrain; on the left, Union Street, which is yours."

"Oh! my God!" said James in a tone of the deepest depression.

"Come on, it's not so bad when you get started," said Rupert encouragingly. "Look, let's meet here again in an hour and compare notes."

"Do you mean we're expected to wander in and out of these hovels for more than an hour?" demanded James.

"Privilege carries its responsibilities," said Rupert solemnly. "Now buck up, James, there's a good chap. It's really quite fun when you get into it."

"All right," said James gloomily, and the two friends started down their respective streets.

* * *

The first three houses James passed without a glance. He just could not bring himself to start on this highly distasteful task. But at the fourth, he muttered to himself. "This will never do." He turned and surveyed the house. The front door opened straight on to the street, its paint blistered and peeling. The window beside it was tightly shut and hung with tattered and grimy lace curtains. James squared his shoulders. Here goes! he said to himself, and he pushed open the door and walked in.

He was in a room that clearly served as bedroom, sitting-room and kitchen for several people. Nearly half of it was taken up by a huge rickety iron bedstead covered with paper-thin blankets and pieces of sacking. On a backless chair sat a man holding a saucepan over a tiny fire that had been made in a broken battered grate. At his feet, a wax-faced baby moaned incessantly in a soap box.

"Good-morning," said James loudly with a brightness he was far from feeling. "What a nice little home you have here, Mr. — Mr. —"

"Ferguson's the name," said the man. He rose slowly from his seat and then, with apparent reluctance, touched his forelock. "Won't you sit down, sir?" he added with an air of resignation.

"Thank you," said James as genially as he could and took the proffered chair. "And now, Mr. Ferguson —"

"If you're from the Guardians," broke in the man with sudden vehemence, "then it's no good, like I've said before. God knows we need help, but I've not asked the Parish for it and I never will."

"Why not?" asked James, too much interested to correct the misapprehension.

"If we accept Parish help, we've got to go into the workhouse, haven't we?" said Mr. Ferguson sullenly. "That's the law, isn't it?"

"Is it?" asked James, and then, as Mr. Ferguson stared at him in surprise, he added, "I'm afraid you're making a mistake. I'm not from the Guardians, as you call it, I'm simply canvassing for the Tory candidate." Mr. Ferguson said nothing and James went on, "I've only just got back from abroad and there's a lot of things I don't understand yet. Why do you need Parish help? Are you unemployed? And if you are, can't you draw the dole?"

Mr. Ferguson's emaciated features twisted into a grimace that might have been meant for a smile. "There's no unemployment now," he said, "and likewise there's no dole. The Tories never liked the dole, you remember. 'Paying the able-bodied man to be idle' you'll remember they called it. So as soon as they got into power, they abolished the dole and revived the Parish Relief."

"How does that work?" asked James.

"If you need help," said Mr. Ferguson, "you can apply to the Board of Guardians for it. And if they grant it, then you and the wife and the kids have all got to go to the workhouse. And since there's nobody would go to the workhouse unless they were on their last legs, well, the Government's sure this way that nobody's going to get relief unless they'd be dead without it. But myself," he added under his breath, "I'd sooner be dead than accept it."

"But a minute ago you said there was no unemployment," said James, somewhat puzzled. "If you're in work, why do you need relief?"

"D'you really want to know?" said Mr. Ferguson doubtfully.

"Yes, I do," said James, and surprisingly he meant it.

"Then I'll tell you," said Mr. Ferguson with an air of one taking a decision. "You take a look at Starveham. You can see it's not been prosperous for years. There used to be mining here, but that all closed down in the twenties, and then we had years of unemployment until just before the last war, a Czech refugee button-manufacturer came and set up a factory here. Well, that did very well. There was full employment, plenty of money coming in, and, with the rationing and the price controls, a man and his kids could be sure of a full belly. Then — the new régime came in." He stopped abruptly.

"Go on," said James encouragingly.

Mr. Ferguson said in an odd voice, "You'll understand I'm not making any complaints. I'm simply telling you what happened because you asked me. See?"

"I see," said James. "Please go on."

Mr. Ferguson continued. "The first thing that happened was that all the rationing stopped and all the controls came off. All of a sudden we found that our money wouldn't hardly buy us enough to eat and the queues stretched from one end of town to the other. Then the factory changed hands. It had been making a lot of money, see, and this Czech it belonged to, they said he wasn't the right type ever to make an A, and all this land belonging to Lord Starveleigh and one thing and another — well, the long and short of it is that they persuaded the Czech to sell it to Lord Starveleigh, and now he's the master."

"That's interesting," exclaimed James, thinking for the moment of his own affairs.

"It was very interesting," said Mr. Ferguson grimly. "Our new master straightway became a member of the International Button-Makers' Cartel — an American organization they tell me, but under German control. The next thing we knew was that Lord Starveleigh had to agree to restrict output. They paid him compensation, of course, but as far as we workers were concerned, it meant half-time work three days a week and that's why," he ended bitterly, "you find me sitting at home of a week-day with nothing to do but mind the baby."

"I suppose," ventured James tentatively, "you don't get much money for that amount of work."

"No," said Mr. Ferguson, I don't. And that's why the missus is out charring at the doctor's house up the hill and that's why my Ada has started in the factory at eleven and that's why we haven't barely a stick of furniture left. And if you're come to ask me to come and cheer for the Tory candidate, well then, I can't say anything but that I'll be there because I can't afford not to be. And now you've got what you've come for, sir, and I'll say good-day to you." And James found himself obediently rising from his chair and out in the street again.

❉   ❉   ❉

Once there he said in a muddled voice: "There's something wrong somewhere." Then he shook himself, aghast. How could there be anything wrong in a world where he and his kind could have such a perfectly marvellous time? It's us or them, I suppose, he said to himself, and somebody's always got to suffer. Then, by a natural train of thought, he began to consider his parents and the plans he was making to thwart them. Somehow or other his conscience didn't feel altogether and entirely easy about them. But one's got to do what's best for people, even if they don't like it, he argued, and he walked a few yards down the street and looked at the next house.

This was even more dilapidated than the one he had just entered. The plaster was peeling off the walls, the door hung askew on its hinges, and the window glass had been broken and roughly mended with lumps of rag stuck through the holes. More like a pigsty than a home, said James to himself, and he took a deep breath and pushed open the door and walked in.

For a moment his eyes, accustomed to the sunlight outside, could discern nothing in the gloom that hung like a pall over the squalid little room. Gradually, he

saw that two figures were squatting by the empty fireplace and that these, as he entered, rose and came
towards him.

And then, "Janice!" he cried aloud. "My God, it's
Janice — and Martin!"

Chapter 12

MARTIN SAID URGENTLY, "Come in quickly, James — and shut the door behind you."

James did as he was told and then, his eyes becoming accustomed to the murk, took a good look at Martin and Janice. The latter, he saw, was still wearing the appalling black clothes he had seen her in in the dock. Her face was lined and haggard and the streak of lipstick across it served only to accentuate this. Martin was wearing a pair of torn flannel trousers and a ragged shirt and on his face was that same look of utter frustration that had so shocked James on the Southampton station platform. But when he spoke it was still in those sardonic tones that had always managed to rile James so effectively on the island.

"Well, James," he said, "you look very well, if I may say so, and exceedingly prosperous. Apparently the new régime agrees with you. And to what do we owe the honour of this visit?"

James stammered. "It was really an accident. I'd no idea — I mean, I was just canvassing — " and then the strangeness of it all overcame him and he asked, "But whatever are you doing here? Last time I saw Janice it was at Great Marlborough Street and I tried to find you afterwards, Janice, but they said you'd gone off with someone — "

"And that someone was me," finished Martin. "My

case was the first on the list that morning — you must
have missed it. I'd been appealing from my original
grading as an E — but it wasn't a spot of good, of
course." He shrugged his shoulders.

"You were graded as an E!" exclaimed James, really
shocked. "However did that happen?"

Martin asked, "You really interested or is that just a
polite inquiry?"

James protested. "No, Martin, really I want to know
— and how you got here — and how you ran into
Janice." There was no doubting his sincerity and, indeed, the last fact at least he wanted to know very
badly.

"All right, then," agreed Martin. "You'd better take
a chair — Oh, no, sorry. There isn't one. Lean against
the wall, James — that is, if you can find a square foot
free from lice."

"I'll stand, thank you," said James with a shudder.
Janice resumed her half-crouching pose by the fireplace; how desirable she was, thought James with a
fierce pang, even in those clothes and this filthy hovel.
Martin was starting his story.

"It was ages before I could get off the ship," he began. "I remember hearing some thunder and thinking
that the storm must have got on everyone's nerves,
because all of a sudden there seemed to be a lot of
pushing and shoving, and every time I made for the
gangway, someone pushed me back. Anyway, in the
end they let me go. I could see Ughtred walking across

the quay and disappearing into some shed place, and I started to follow him. But when I got to the entrance, there was some bloody official standing by the entrance who wouldn't let me in. 'You go next door,' he said, looking me up and down in an impertinent sort of way, and he jerked his thumb to the next shed which had got a great B stuck over the door.

"Mind you," he went on, "I didn't realize then that anything funny had happened. I didn't like the man's manner, but I just thought that the first shed was full or something. So I walked across to the next one and went in."

"Did they give you a drink?" asked James curiously.

Martin started. "Good God, no!" he said in surprise. "There were some benches round the walls upholstered in a kind of imitation leather and a lot of gaudy railway posters. But no drinks. And I could have done with one by then. Anyway, after I'd waited about ten minutes, I was sent for to a little room with a uniformed official in it. He started by being quite polite – gave me a hard chair, asked if I was comfortable, and then wanted my name, address, job and so on. I told him all that, and he wrote it down on a form. Then all of a sudden he said, 'Do you like Picasso?'

"I was a bit startled," said Martin, "but at the same time I must admit I was rather thrilled. I mean, one of the things we'd hoped socialism would do would be to give everyone a taste for Art and all that, and I remember thinking it was rather touching that this fellow was so interested that he even wanted to have a discussion with a complete stranger."

"And do you like Picasso?" asked James interestedly.

"As a matter of fact," said Martin, "I don't. I very much prefer Rouault or even Bracque. But I wanted to encourage the man, so I said, with as much enthusiasm as I could muster, 'I think he's absolutely superb; in fact, I should say he was far and away the greatest painter of our epoch.'

"The man looked at me oddly. He said, 'Are you quite sure that's what you think?' And, fool that I was, I thought this was rather pathetic, that he wanted to be quite certain that my opinion endorsed his own. So I said, 'Of course that's what I think. I'll say it on oath if you like.'

"Do you know," said Martin, "I believe it was then that I first had the notion that something very funny had happened. The man looked at me so oddly. Then he laid down his pen and said, 'Well, you've done for yourself properly, young man. If you hadn't been so vehement, I might have fixed you up at Aberystwyth like we did Mr. Rowse. But after what you said about Picasso, I've got no choice. You're for the E's.'

"I didn't know what he was talking about. I said, 'What the hell do you mean?' and then he explained. He was quite decent — but it was such a shock to me I barely took it in. Then he sent me along to the E shed, a filthy hole where they herded us like cattle and made us queue for hours."

"I saw you on the platform," remarked James. "I thought you looked pretty depressed."

"I was," said Martin, "and so would you have been. Everything I'd dreamt of, everything I'd hoped for — all suddenly gone."

James said, "Well, if you'd got the régime you wanted, it would have been like that for me."

For a moment they glared at each other. Then Martin shrugged his shoulders. "Want to hear the rest of it?" he asked.

"Please," said James apologetically.

"It's soon told," said Martin. "I got to London in a foul slow train that stopped everywhere. I couldn't find an hotel to take me in, so I slept on the Embankment. Next day, I went to a Ministry Office in Stepney they'd told me to go to. Here I learnt what being an E means."

James asked, "What does it mean?"

"Most importantly," replied Martin, "it means that you can't become a member of a Trade Union and unless you're a member of a Trade Union you can't take a regular job. Apparently," he added, "the Unions insisted on this as their price for supporting the régime. Well, I protested, of course. I protested like mad. And in the end they told me I could appeal to become a D.

"So I appealed. But it wasn't any good. My remarks about Picasso had completely ditched me. I met Janice at the court and we agreed we'd stick together. After

all, we were both derelict and we'd always got on quite
well — and here we are. Got a cigarette?"

"Of course," said James, hurriedly pulling out his
case and offering it round. Janice coughed as she lit
hers and said, "Funny how strong they seem when
you're not used to them."

"Have you given up smoking?" asked James.

"We couldn't afford it," said Martin briefly.

James looked round the grim little room and with a
sudden shock asked, "But how do you live?"

Janice said sullenly, "There's only one way a female
E can live."

"And she very kindly keeps me as well," said Martin,
blowing the smoke through his nose. "And now you
know all about it."

"But I don't," expostulated James in some bewilderment. "Why did you come here to Starveham?"

"I was sent," said Martin, with an inscrutable expression on his face.

James suddenly understood. He exclaimed, "You're
underground. But you can't be! Socialists don't go
underground; they compromise."

"Quite," agreed Martin, "and that's why I'm not a
Socialist any more. I'm a Communist. And they don't
compromise."

"But look here," argued James, "you're wasting your
time. The régime is firmly established; it's liked by
everyone; and nothing further from a Communist régime could possibly be imagined."

"That," said Martin, "is just where you're wrong. Nothing in the world would be easier than to change this régime into a Communist one. It's just a question of redistributing the discs."

"I don't understand," said James, bewildered.

"In any hierarchical society," said Martin impatiently, "some such system as this prevails. The only difference between this system and the Russian one is which people are at the bottom and which are at the top."

Janice suddenly broke in. "For God's sake, quit arguing politics. There's a lot of things I want to ask James. How's Penelope and how's Ughtred?"

On an impulse James asked, "Would you like to see them both?"

For the first time since his arrival a look of eagerness and animation came into their faces. "I'll say we would," breathed Janice, and James with patronizing benevolence said, "All right. I'll see if I can bring them along this evening. But it would be pretty late," he added, thinking hurriedly, "They don't dine till late at Starveleigh Castle."

"That'll be all right," said Martin sardonically. "Janice doesn't knock off till pretty late either."

Again James remembered how very much he had always disliked Martin. He was about to speak, but at that moment a voice was heard shouting outside in the street. "James!" it was calling, "James!" louder and louder as it came nearer.

James started. "That's my colleague looking for me,"

he said hurriedly. "I must be off. Look out for us late this evening."

He rose and made for the door. Janice said pleadingly, "You won't let anything stop you bringing them, will you, James?" and James said earnestly, "No, I won't. I promise," and slipped out to meet Rupert.

*　　*　　*

"I was just a little worried when you didn't turn up," Rupert said. "The workers are said to be pretty well disciplined and all that, but after all, one never knows, does one?"

"Oh, I was all right," said James quickly. "I just got interested, that was all."

"You didn't manage to work very far down the street," Rupert said with a certain suspicion in his voice. "I hope, James, you didn't let yourself get *familiar*."

"Naturally not!" said James stiffly, with as much coldness as he could muster, and Rupert said apologetically. "Sorry, James. What I really came to tell you is that they've got some lunch waiting for us at the Committee Rooms." "Good show!" commented James, and they walked amicably back together.

*　　*　　*

At the Committee Rooms a hilarious party was in progress. Lord Starveleigh's servants had brought down from the Castle ample hampers of provisions and lashings of champagne, and all the company was

merrily relaxing from its morning exertions. Dexter-
ously giving Rupert the slip, James seized a leg of cold
pheasant and made his way to a remote corner, where
he had seen Ughtred and Penelope talking absorbedly
together.

They broke off as he approached and greeted him
warmly, but somehow he had the odd idea that he
wasn't altogether welcome. They all three began to
talk about the election and their several experiences
that morning, but James had the feeling that the conversation he had interrupted was on quite a different
topic.

He said suddenly, "I want you to promise to do something for me."

Ughtred began, "Anything I can do — " and Penelope asked, "What is it, James?"

"I want you two," said James urgently, "to slip away
when the rest of the party goes off to bed, and meet me
outside. I want to take you and show you something
terrifically interesting."

Ughtred said doubtfully, "Well, I don't know — "

James broke in, "It really is most frightfully important or I wouldn't ask you."

His tone and manner seemed to impress them. Penelope looked at Ughtred and said, "All right. I'll meet
you by the gazebo when the others have gone to bed."

"I'll be there, too," Ughtred promised and James said
earnestly, "I assure you it will be worth your while."

❋   ❋   ❋

All through the afternoon's canvassings, the drive home, the interminable dinner, James hugged his plan with deep secret joy. It was, as far as he could see, satisfactory on every possible count. As far as Janice and Martin were concerned, it should do them both a world of good thus to be visited by their former companions under the aegis of James himself. Martin should finally realize, James told himself gloatingly, that birth and breeding were the only things that had the slightest importance. And as for his former patronage of Penelope — well, it should sting him to the heart to see her now in her new-found glory and realize that not he but James had got her. Janice was a different proposition, but James was determined that the same factors should act in her case. Seeing him in all the magnificence of his present success, she surely could not fail to realize the contrast between the James she had so contemptuously rejected on the island and this one, successfully carrying off the catch of the season. If I can offer her anything better than that foul hovel, she'll soon see reason, James assured himself. If necessary, he was even prepared to inform on Martin's activities to ensure his removal from the scene; but he was determined not to lose sight of Janice again.

As for Ughtred, James had been somewhat puzzled and disconcerted by his attitude during the past twenty-four hours. Ughtred had not seemed at all his genial happy self, had rather behaved as though he was desperately worried over something and striving to reach a decision. James felt, rather than thought, that it would do Ughtred good to see something of the contrasts to A existence.

But the real crux of James's plan was to be its effect on Penelope. As far as he was concerned, it was clearly imperative from every point of view that she should be persuaded to consent to an immediate and public engagement. But somehow or other, up to the present, he had been afraid to press her. True, she had agreed in principle to marry him. Yet always James had the uncomfortable feeling that he was a *pis aller,* and that Penelope's real inclinations were still directed elsewhere. But if she should see Martin as he is now, James gloated, dirty and ragged and unkempt, natural reaction should throw her straight into my arms, and I ought to be able to persuade her to agree to a public engagement right away. And if we could announce it in front of the whole house party, he reflected, I don't believe even old Featherstonehaugh would be able to do anything about it. He turned the plan over and over in his mind, and every way he looked at it he found it was good.

❂   ❂   ❂

"I've got the Lagonda waiting in the drive," James whispered. "I hope you're warmly wrapped up, Penny." He looked at the loose velvet cloak she had thrown over her white satin frock.

"I'll be all right," she answered somewhat impatiently, but James, still punctilious for the comfort of his guests, asked solicitously, "And you, Ughtred?"

With a thick raglan overcoat over his dinner jacket, a muffler round his neck and a tweed cap pulled down over his forehead, Ughtred certainly looked well wrapped against the inclemencies of the night air. "I shall be perfectly warm, I assure you, James," he now answered. "But I trust you are not taking us too far."

"Only to Starveham," James replied reassuringly, and he led them across the grass to where his car was waiting under a huge chestnut. He had remembered to bring rugs and now he tucked these carefully round their knees and they started off.

No words were exchanged between them on the short journey to the town. James was too much oppressed with stiffled excitement to offer any light remark, and the three of them kept silence until at last in the glittering moonlight they drew up before the hovel in Union Street.

James helped them out of the car, and now Ughtred said anxiously, "I trust, James, you are having some care where you are taking us."

"It's perfectly all right," said James reassuringly, and he pushed open the door and motioned them to enter.

Then — "Janice!" cried Ughtred, and "Martin!" cried Penelope, and in an instant they were all entangled in each other's arms.

❀　　❀　　❀

Martin loosened his grip of Penelope and said, "Now we must all get away as quickly as we can."

"I quite agree," said Ughtred. "Where shall we go?"

"What about Scotland?" suggested Penelope in her old timid voice. "I've heard that what with being so well educated and so on, they haven't taken to the new régime like we have here."

"Or America?" said Janice hopefully looking from one to the other.

"No," said Martin curtly. "Neither of these will do. America's too far and Scotland's not far enough."

"I know," said Ughtred with sudden excitement. "We'll go to Eire. They tell me that's where all English refugees are going nowadays."

"Eire it is," said Martin decisively, and the women made eager noises of assent.

"But look here," shouted James suddenly. "Look here! What do you think you're all doing? You must be mad!"

The others stared at him silently.

"Penny!" James cried. "Have you forgotten? Penny, you're going to marry me!"

"No," said Penelope. "I'm going to marry Martin. You see, we love each other."

"But, Penny," screamed James, "think of all you're giving up. Look at Martin! You can't want to share your life with *that*."

"But I do," said Penelope, and she looked up at

Martin with a smile of exquisite sweetness, and he bent down and kissed her again.

"You must be mad," James said desperately. He swung round. "Ughtred," he cried. "*You* tell her — "

"I can't, James, I'm afraid," said Ughtred, smiling a little sadly. "You see, I'm mad, too."

"But, Ughtred," begged James, "what's happened to you? I thought you were so happy under the new régime?"

"I was," said Ughtred, "until yesterday morning."

Martin asked curiously, "What happened then?"

"I discovered," said Ughtred, "that the press was no longer free. You will think it strange, no doubt, Martin, that I can swallow what must seem to you so many camels and boggle at one gnat, but I look at these things differently. I have always been a Conservative. I have always believed in privilege. I have always believed in the natural superiority of one class and that my own; I have always believed that this class alone was by nature fitted to govern. But equally I have always believed, fundamentally and decisively, in the freedom of the British press."

"But look here," cried James despairingly, "you just *couldn't* have a free press now. I mean if you did, you'd have all the intellectuals writing for it and, if they did, they'd all be putting forward progressive views and then you'd never have a sound Tory government."

"That," said Ughtred very sadly, "is just what I am

beginning to realize." He turned to Martin. "We'd better get moving," he said.

"I think so, too," Martin agreed quietly. "Well, we're ready. There's nothing Janice and I want to take."

At the mention of Janice, James tried one last appeal. "Ughtred," he cried, "Ughtred, you don't want to go off with Janice! What about the widow in Park Village East?"

Ughtred turned to Janice and tucked her arm in his. "Janice and I have always got on very well together," he said, and Janice squeezed his arm and agreed, "That's right, Ughtred. I could listen to you talking for ever."

"I suppose," Ughtred said hesitatingly to James, "you wouldn't think of coming with us?"

"Like hell I would," shouted James. "I'm sticking to what I've got. You others can go off and make fools of yourselves — I'll have the laugh of you in the end."

"James," said Ughtred very quietly, "I quite agree that the odds are against us, that it is more than likely that you will, as you put it, have the laugh of us in the end. But I am going to appeal to you, in the name of our old comradeship, to give us what help you can in making our getaway."

"Oh, all right," said James sulkily, "what can I do?"

Ughtred told him.

*　　*　　*

Ten minutes later Martin was wearing James's

smartly cut dinner jacket and James was in Martin's old rags. "You'd better let him have your disc, too," Ughtred urged. "With a gold one, Martin can take Janice anywhere and no questions asked." There was something in Ughtred's manner that commanded obedience and James handed his disc over without a word.

"Now," said Ughtred solemnly, "we must be going. With your Lagonda we should be at Holyhead before day breaks and I will leave instructions there that the car is to be returned to you. And now, James, one last word. Can we rely on you to say nothing to anyone about our departure until we are safe in Ireland?"

"I'm not a sneak," said James indignantly.

"Remember," said Ughtred, still more solemnly, "our safety is in your hands. We all of us rely on your loyalty. Good-bye, James."

"Good-bye," echoed the others and they passed out of the door, Janice on Ughtred's arm, Penelope encircled by Martin's and on all their faces a look of complete fulfilment and happiness.

And then James heard the roar of the Lagonda dying away in the distance and then silence fell and he was all alone.

*　　*　　*

For some time he crouched by the fire with his head in his hands, utterly disconsolate, utterly bereft. His plan was shattered to fragments, his every dream dashed to the ground. He thought of the hopes he had built on his marriage to Penelope. He remembered the

happy lunches with Ughtred at his club. He remembered, too, those gay bachelor evenings with Rupert
and realized bitterly how the action of those four, who
had once been his friends, would have bereft him even
of that, for what chance had he now of retaining his
own status when the one weapon he had hoped to use
against his parents' plan had been torn from his grasp.
Suddenly he leapt to his feet and shouted aloud, "I
won't stand it! I won't stand it!"

But how to stop it? What could he do but humour
his unspoken promise to Ughtred, sit there, silent and
impotent, until the others had made their escape, and
then return alone to his inevitable degradation?

What could he do? What could he do He could do
one thing that would undoubtedly and certainly safeguard himself and his own future.

He could tell.

"It's my duty, he told himself frantically, it's my duty
to the régime. Personal loyalties must give way to
higher ones. It's my duty to tell, to get them stopped,
to stop them ratting on the régime — and, by proving
my loyalty, to safeguard my own position, save myself.
Without letting himself consider any further, he rushed
madly out of the door and along the streets, up the hill
to Starveleigh Castle.

❋   ❋   ❋

"I'll go straight to Featherstonehaugh," he told himself, as he rushed along in his rags. "I'll see they don't

get away with it. They've got no right to get away with it. Why should they all get out and be happy? I'll go straight to Featherstonehaugh and he'll see I'm loyal and then — " and on he rushed, panting heavily, up the hill.

The lodge gates were shut. Unseeing, James fell against them, bruising his hands, and then clung on to them, shaking them savagely. "Let me through," he shouted. "Let me through!"

A light snapped on in the lodge and a window jerked open. James could see the rosy-cheeked woman looking down on him.

"Let me through!" he screamed. "Open the gates, I tell you. Let me through at once!"

"In those rags!" said the woman, and laughed derisively. "You'd better go home to bed, my man, if you don't want to find yourself in the lock-up."

"But I'm one of the house-guests!" screamed James, and then, with a desperate attempt at the minatory tone of a master, "Look here, my good woman, you'll find yourself in pretty serious trouble if you take to treating Lord Starveleigh's guests in this way."

In the act of closing the window, the woman seemed to hesitate and then to make up her mind. "You wait there a minute," she said briefly, "I'll come down."

Waiting, James laughed in weak relief. "That's the way to treat the lower classes," he encouraged himself. "Put the fear of God into them, and you'll soon have them cringing to lick your hand."

But there wasn't much sign of cringing about the lodgekeeper when she finally descended in a red flannel wrapper and beckoned James to the honeysuckle-hung porch. "Now if you're one of the castle guests, like you say you are," she began in a tone clearly determined to brook no nonsense, "I take it you'll have no objection to showing me your disc, just to make sure everything's in order, like."

"Naturally not," said James haughtily — and then remembered. He had given his disc to Martin, to the hated abhorrant Martin, to carry Martin to safety with Penelope. It could not be borne! The moment was too tense for anger and wild tempestuous raving. He said to the woman with a quietness that carried conviction, "Owing to circumstances over which I have no control, my disc is not at this moment in my possession. But that is beside the point. What is vitally important is that I should speak to Mr. Featherstonehaugh at the Castle at the earliest possible moment, and I warn you that in impeding me, you are failing in your duty to the social system."

The woman seemed impressed. She stood for a moment in indecision and then said, "I'll tell you what I'll do. I can't let you through in those rags and without no disc; it 'ud be as much as my grade was worth. But I'll ring up the Castle and tell this Mr. Featherstonehaugh that you're here, and more than that I cannot do."

"All right," said James, recognising finality in her

voice and he waited, leaning against the porch, while she went into the lodge, closing the door carefully behind her. He heard the telephone bell tinkle and waited in a numbness of apprehension until the woman came back and said expressionlessly, "You're to wait here. Mr. Featherstonehaugh said he'd be along," and then shut the door again.

In the still summer night under the myriad stars James walked again to the huge iron gates and there waited, clutching the bars that stood between him and Starveleigh Castle. He was beyond thought now, almost beyond conscious apprehension, his whole being consumed with the one urgent desire, to get back — back to safety and security and the standards of his peers.

Then in the darkness he heard a softly whispered "James!" and Rupert Crooke-Haughton stood before him on the other side of the gate.

"Oh, James!" said Rupert in a voice fraught with infinite sadness, and then he seemed overpowered and was silent.

"Oh, Rupert!" breathed James in infinite relief, "Rupert, you've come to let me in."

"No, James," said Rupert, and then the silence of the night was broken by the sound of a car engine coming nearer and nearer. "That's Featherstonehaugh," whispered Rupert, and then, like the last breath of an expiring ghost, James heard him say, "I've come to say — good-bye, James."

"Rupert!" shrieked James, but there was no answer. Rupert had gone, and before James there was only the beam of the headlights as the car rapidly approached him.

❊   ❊   ❊

The car stopped. Mr. Featherstonehaugh descended and walked slowly and with awful majesty to the gates.

"Featherstonehaugh," gasped James hysterically, "Featherstonehaugh, let me in, quick. I've got very important information for you. When I've told you, you'll see what a good A I am. I haven't been thinking about anything but the good of the régime, really I haven't. Featherstonehaugh, let me in."

But Mr. Featherstonehaugh had stopped on the other side of the gates. He made no move to open them, only waited silent and immobile until James's frenetic babblings had died away into terrified silence. Then he spoke.

"It's no use," he said. "You've been purged."

"Purged!" repeated James wildly, "Purged! In God's name why? I'm loyal!"

"You have been purged," Mr. Featherstonehaugh stated, "for the usual reason. You have been associating with people who don't think like we do," and then, moved, perhaps, to compassion by the sight of James's devastated face, he added, "Come now, what else could you have expected? There isn't a civilised state in the world today that doesn't purge people who mix with people who don't think right." He turned to the car. "Perkins," he called, "the bags."

From the shadows emerged a footman carrying what James with a fresh thrill of horror recognised as his luggage. "Throw them over," ordered Mr. Featherstonehaugh, and one by one his bags curved a tidy parabola over the gate and landed in the road beside him. An act apparently so irrevocable roused James to a final effort.

"But, Featherstonehaugh," he wailed, "what shall I do? What shall I do?"

Mr. Featherstonehaugh said quietly, "We are not vindictive. We understand that your misdemeanour is due to weakness rather than roguery. But you have acted in a deviationist manner, and it is an essential tenet of our beliefs that the Upper-Class Line must be rigorously adhered to. So you have been summarily degraded to the rank of B, and I trust," he added firmly, "that no further steps will have to be taken."

"But that's illegal," gasped James in horror, "You can't degrade me like that. You've got to take it before the courts."

Suddenly Mr. Featherstonehaugh laughed. "Legal," he roared, and he nearly bent double with mirth, "Legal! You fool. You don't even know the first thing about contemporary life. Whatever benefits the State is legal and if it isn't today, a retrogressive — I mean, retrospective — law will see that it is tomorrow. Legal!"

And he laughed himself nearly sick and then prepared to turn away.

But James, his last vestige of control gone, was shrieking his final defiance through the gates. "You — you — " he spluttered as he sought for words venemous enough for this ultimate expression of the hate and frustration of James Leigh-Smith. "You stinking little twerp." He said.

Mr. Featherstonehaugh turned back and drew himself up to his full height. "Smith," he said icily, "Smith, you forget yourself."

*　　*　　*

THE END

Persephone Books publishes the following titles: